Sorceline

SYLVIA DOUYÉ

Illustrated by
PAOLA ANTISTA

Andrews McMeel
PUBLISHING®

Part 1

Welcome to the Isle of Vorn! Everything here is creepy, gloomy, and super scary. In other words, deadly cool! Exactly what I need.

My name is Sorceline and I've come here to study cryptozoology. Ya heard of it?

It's the study of cryptids: amazing creatures that most humans don't think exist.

I got a summer apprenticeship with Archibald Balzar—a zoologist who specializes in them.

So now my days will be spent learning to tell elves from fairies . . .

. . . and searching the countryside for unicorns.

Or I'll be studying how a dragon breathes fire . . .

!

. . . and what it eats!

EACH ONE OF YOU HAS COME HERE FULL OF AMBITION . . .

. . . YOU ALL DREAM OF BECOMING SPECIALISTS IN LEGENDARY CREATURES.

SO, TAKE A LOOK AROUND AND SAY HELLO TO THE COMPETITION!

AFTER WE HAVE SPENT A CERTAIN NUMBER OF HOURS TOGETHER . . .

. . . I WILL SELECT THE BEST ONE OF YOU TO BE MY ASSISTANT. BUT BEFORE THEN, THERE ARE A FEW RULES YOU'LL NEED TO FOLLOW.

RULE NUMBER 1:

NEVER ARRIVE LATE TO MY CLASS!

5

I'M SORRY . . . I . . . UH . . .

IT WAS MY GUIDE . . . UH . . . MY TAXI . . . HE WAS EATEN BY A . . .

EXPLAIN THAT TO THE CREATURE THAT DIES BECAUSE YOU DIDN'T GET THERE IN TIME!

IT WON'T CARE ABOUT WHY YOU'RE LATE. NOW TAKE YOUR SEAT!

PROFESSOR, COME QUICK!

RULE NUMBER TWO: WHEN THERE'S AN EMERGENCY, DROP EVERYTHING AND FOLLOW ME!

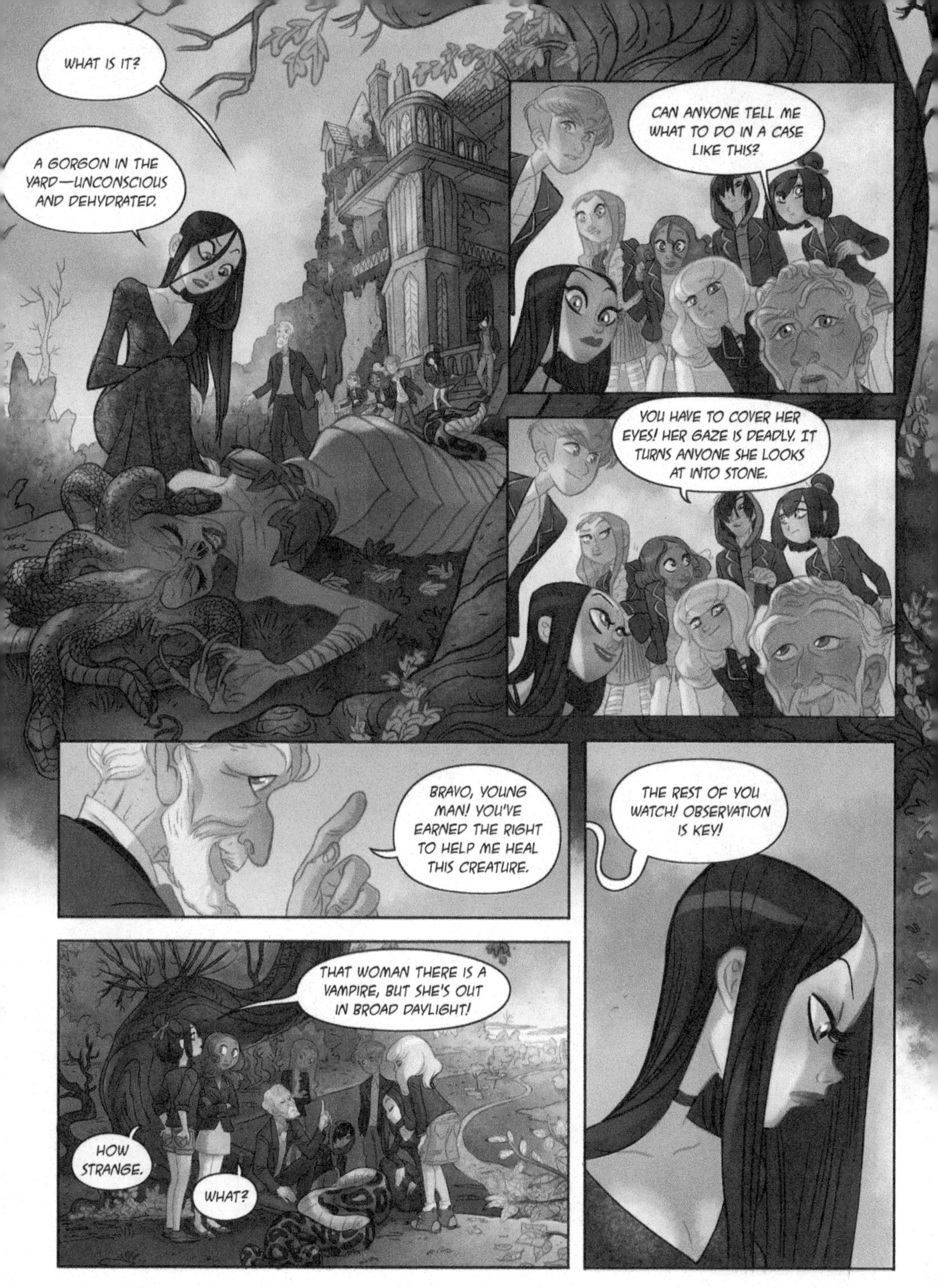
WHAT IS IT?
A GORGON IN THE YARD—UNCONSCIOUS AND DEHYDRATED.
CAN ANYONE TELL ME WHAT TO DO IN A CASE LIKE THIS?
YOU HAVE TO COVER HER EYES! HER GAZE IS DEADLY. IT TURNS ANYONE SHE LOOKS AT INTO STONE.
BRAVO, YOUNG MAN! YOU'VE EARNED THE RIGHT TO HELP ME HEAL THIS CREATURE.
THE REST OF YOU WATCH! OBSERVATION IS KEY!
THAT WOMAN THERE IS A VAMPIRE, BUT SHE'S OUT IN BROAD DAYLIGHT!
HOW STRANGE.
WHAT?

IT'S NOT HARD TO RECOGNIZE A VAMPIRE!

IN BROAD DAYLIGHT IT IS, SINCE THEY'RE NOCTURNAL!

JUST ADMIT IT. SHE'S REALLY GOOD. YOU CAN SEE RIGHT AWAY THAT SHE'S BRILLIANT.

!

I REALLY DON'T KNOW HOW I KNEW!

WELL, IF YOU CAN IDENTIFY CREATURES JUST BY LOOKING AT THEM, THEN YOU'VE DEFINITELY CHOSEN THE RIGHT CAREER!

. . . AND INCREDIBLY CHARMING. THE FIRST TIME SHE LOOKED AT ME I . . . I . . .

I . . . UH . . .

HEHE!

WHAT? WHAT IS IT?

AND COULD YOU TELL RIGHT AWAY HE WAS A KNIGHT IN SHINING ARMOR?

LOOKS LIKE I HAVE A COMPETITOR.

SO, HOW WAS IT? WAS IT EASY TO CURE THE GORGON? YOU MUST'VE LOVED IT!

YOU KNOW, I HAVE A WAY OF DEALING WITH HER HAIR.

I CAN TELL YOU IF YOU WANT!

YOU'RE SO LUCKY THAT YOU GET TO HEAL A GORGON.

WHAT'S IT LIKE?

TELL US!

DON'T BE SHY!

WE'RE ALL HERE TO LEARN.

WOW, TALK ABOUT A COLD SHOULDER!

YEAH, FREEZING. HOW RUDE!

DOES EVERYONE HAVE A BIRD?

I CAN'T BELIEVE I'M HOLDING A PHOENIX. UNREAL!

YOU MUST TAKE VERY GOOD CARE OF THESE ANIMALS. THEY'LL HELP YOU WITH YOUR DIAGNOSES.

OH, COME ON. THAT'S NOT A PHOENIX, THERE'S ONLY ONE ON EARTH AT A TIME AND THERE ARE A BUNCH OF THESE.

WHO KNOWS WHAT KIND OF BIRDS THESE ARE?

I THINK THEY'RE SIMURGHS. THEY HAVE TREMENDOUS HEALING POWERS. THAT'S WHY THEY'LL BE SO HELPFUL.

NO, A SIMURGH IS A HUGE, EAGLE-LIKE BIRD THAT RANGES IN COLOR FROM BROWN TO RED.

THIS BIRD IS SNOW-WHITE AND ONLY A LITTLE LARGER THAN A CROW. I'D GUESS A CALADRIUS.

YES, OF COURSE!

IT'S A CALADRIUS, PROFESSOR BALZAR!

VERY GOOD, TARA!

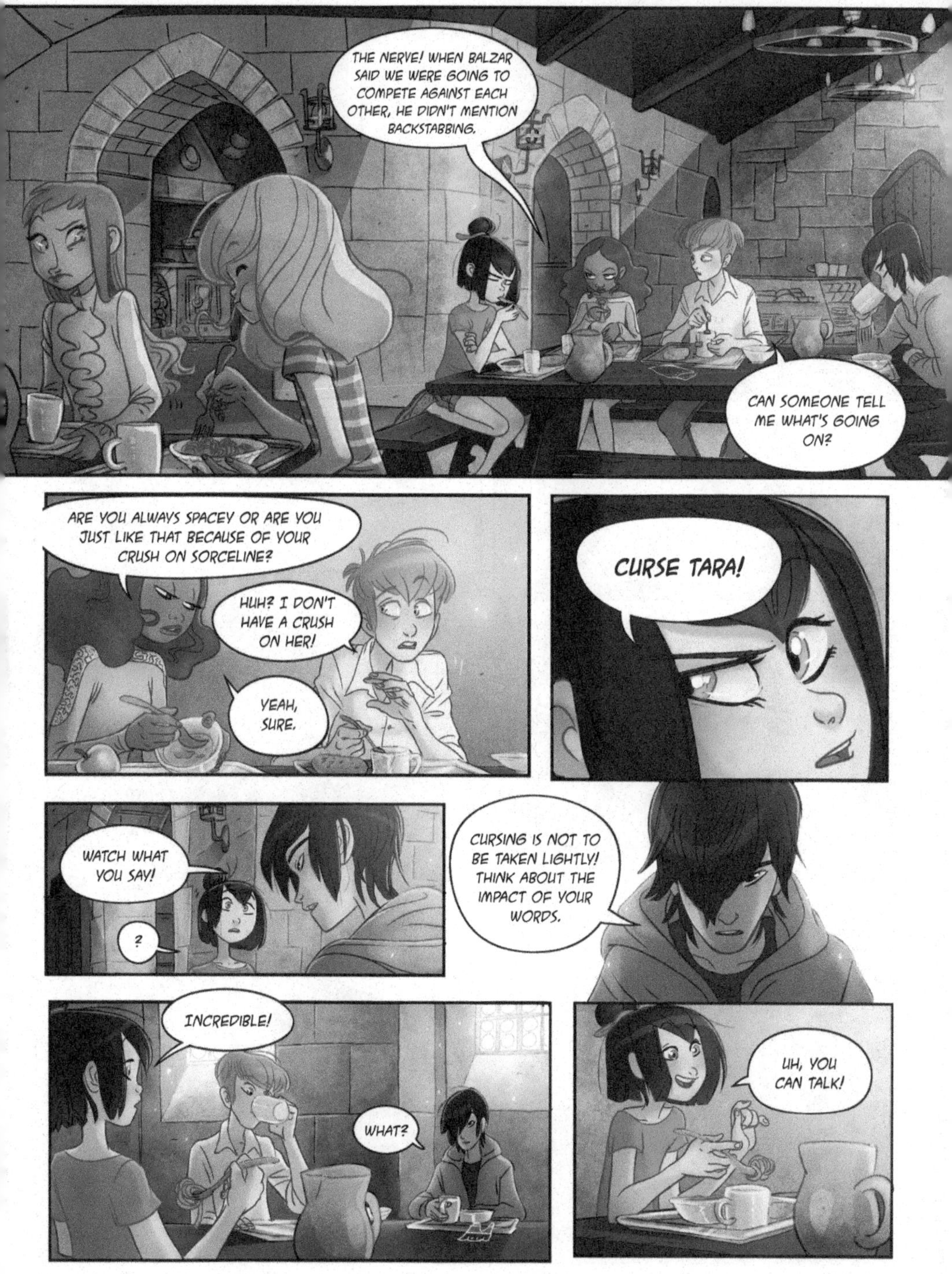
THE NERVE! WHEN BALZAR SAID WE WERE GOING TO COMPETE AGAINST EACH OTHER, HE DIDN'T MENTION BACKSTABBING.
CAN SOMEONE TELL ME WHAT'S GOING ON?
ARE YOU ALWAYS SPACEY OR ARE YOU JUST LIKE THAT BECAUSE OF YOUR CRUSH ON SORCELINE?
HUH? I DON'T HAVE A CRUSH ON HER!
YEAH, SURE.
CURSE TARA!
WATCH WHAT YOU SAY!
?
CURSING IS NOT TO BE TAKEN LIGHTLY! THINK ABOUT THE IMPACT OF YOUR WORDS.
INCREDIBLE!
WHAT?
UH, YOU CAN TALK!

THEY HAD SPAGHETTI BOLOGNESE.

YOU'RE SPOILING THEM...

AND YOU'RE TOO HARD ON THEM...

I HAVE TO BE IF I WANT TO TURN THEM INTO GOOD HEALERS.

A BIT OF TENDERNESS NEVER HURT ANYONE...

BE SURE TO APPLY PLENTY OF SUNSCREEN OR YOU'LL BURN AT THE SLIGHTEST EXPOSURE.

I CAN'T WAIT UNTIL YOUR YOUNG APPRENTICES EXAMINE ME AND FIND OUT I'M A VAMPIRE.

IT'S ONE OF MY FAVORITE MOMENTS.

I HOPE ONE OF THEM IS ABLE TO IDENTIFY YOU. IT'S ONE OF THE WAYS I RECOGNIZE REAL TALENT!

AND NOW WHAT DO WE DO?

BALZAR LEFT INSTRUCTIONS!

WE'RE SUPPOSED TO DETERMINE HOW THE PATIENT'S GOING TO DO . . .

WITH A CALADRIUS, THAT COULDN'T BE EASIER!

EXACTLY. THE BIRD CAN TELL YOU IF THE PATIENT WILL LIVE OR DIE.

BRING THE CALADRIUS CLOSE TO HER. IF IT LOOKS AT HER FACE, SHE'LL LIVE.

WITH ITS GAZE, IT'LL TAKE ON HER ILLNESS AND FLY OFF WITH IT.

BUT IF IT TURNS AWAY . . .

OH NO!

SHE'S GOING TO DIE!

MAYBE THERE'S STILL HOPE. WE NEED SOME UNICORN BLOOD.

WE'LL GO OUT TONIGHT AFTER DINNER. DON'T BE LATE . . .

I FEEL LIKE I'M A CHARACTER IN SOME HORROR MOVIE.

THIS IS NOT THE TIME TO GO FOR A WALK IN THE WOODS. I'D RATHER BE IN BED.

UNICORNS ONLY WALK IN THE WOODS AT NIGHT.

BUT WE CAN'T SEE ANYTHING!

INSTEAD OF STICKING TOGETHER WE SHOULD MAKE TWO GROUPS!

YOU CAN'T MISS THEM, THEY'RE SUCH A BRIGHT WHITE COLOR.

BUT THEY MOVE SO QUICKLY, IT'S DIFFICULT TO TRACK THEM.

BE CAREFUL, THEIR HORNS MAKE THEM DANGEROUS.

YEAH, I KNOW, THE HORN IS REALLY SHARP.

EXACTLY . . . YOU SEE, YOU DO KNOW THINGS ABOUT UNICORNS!

NO, IT'S JUST THAT I FOUND ONE!

HA! IF YOU HAD, IT WOULD HAVE CHARGED US BY NOW!

OH! LOOK AT THAT!

WHAT IS IT?

PIXIES. TINY FAIRIES!

BUT THEY LOOK STRANGE.

YEAH, THEY LOOK LIKE ZOMBIES.

THUD

OUCH!

SHHH! YOU'LL FRIGHTEN THEM.

C'MON!

ALL RIGHT, SINCE WE HAVEN'T FOUND A UNICORN!

BUT . . . IT WAS—

AAAHHH!

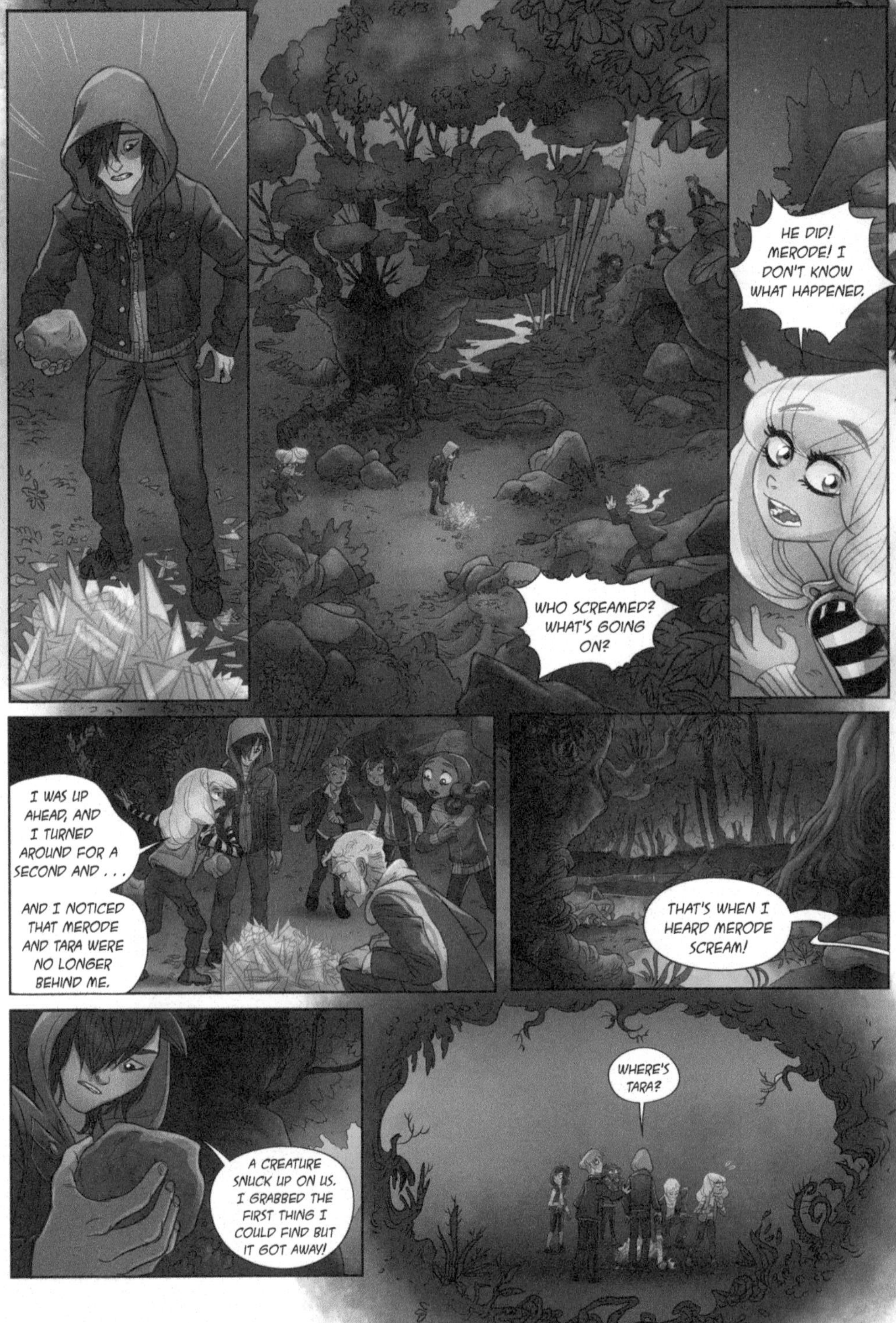
WHO SCREAMED? WHAT'S GOING ON?
HE DID! MERODE! I DON'T KNOW WHAT HAPPENED.
I WAS UP AHEAD, AND I TURNED AROUND FOR A SECOND AND . . .
AND I NOTICED THAT MERODE AND TARA WERE NO LONGER BEHIND ME.
THAT'S WHEN I HEARD MERODE SCREAM!
A CREATURE SNUCK UP ON US. I GRABBED THE FIRST THING I COULD FIND BUT IT GOT AWAY!
WHERE'S TARA?

I'LL GO LOOK FOR HER . . .

I'LL SEARCH ALL NIGHT IF I HAVE TO, BUT I'LL FIND HER!

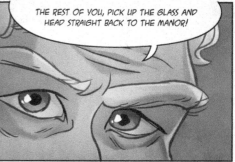

THE REST OF YOU, PICK UP THE GLASS AND HEAD STRAIGHT BACK TO THE MANOR!

PROFESSOR BALZAR! WE CAME ACROSS SOME PIXIES A LITTLE WHILE AGO. MAYBE THEY HAVE SOMETHING TO DO WITH TARA'S DISAPPEARANCE . . .

PIXIES? IMPOSSIBLE! THEY NEVER COME OUT AT NIGHT!

BUT . . .

UH . . . OK! UH, WE'LL GO BACK THEN . . .

YES, AND HURRY!

17

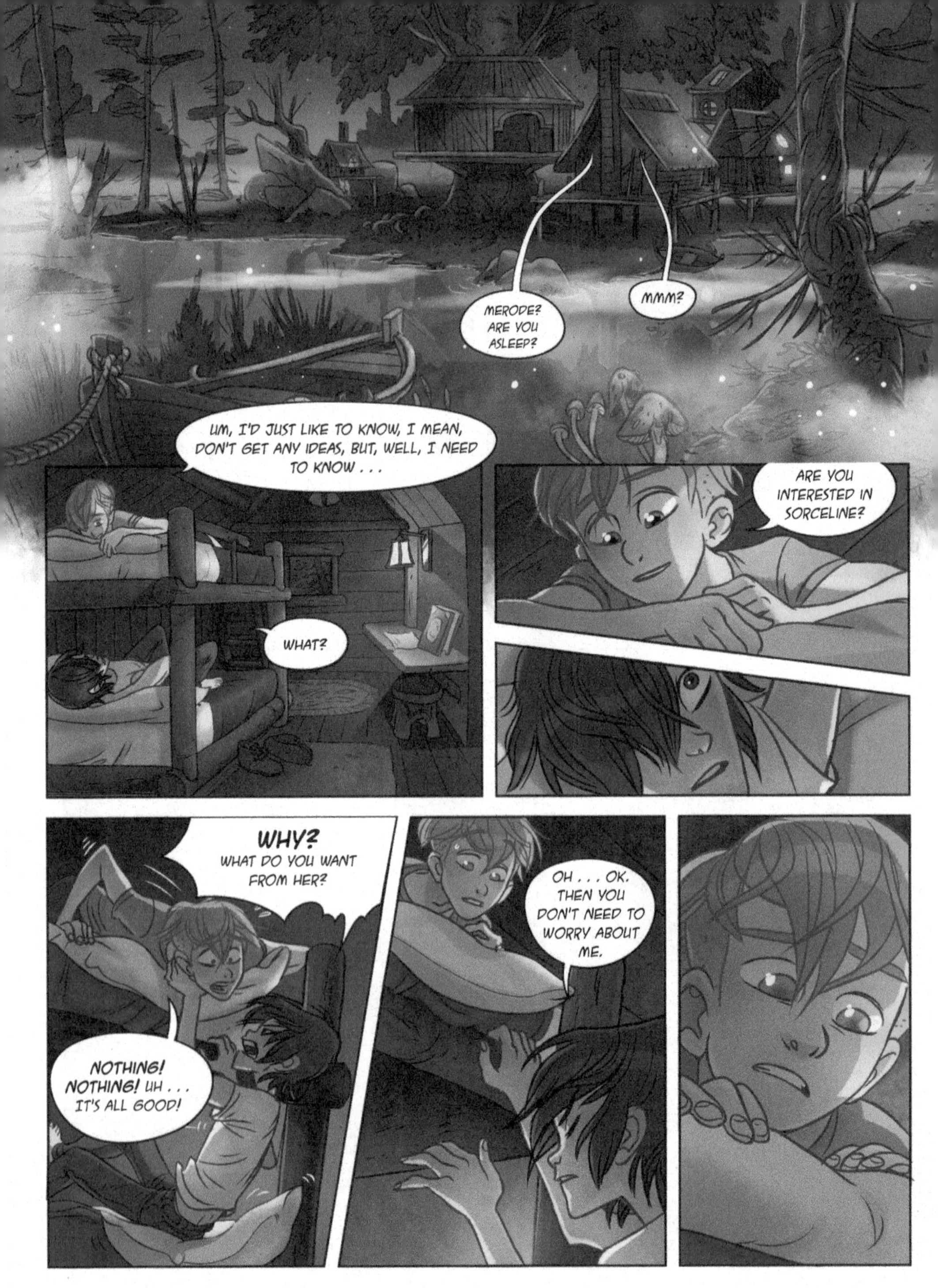
MERODE? ARE YOU ASLEEP?
MMM?
UM, I'D JUST LIKE TO KNOW, I MEAN, DON'T GET ANY IDEAS, BUT, WELL, I NEED TO KNOW . . .
WHAT?
ARE YOU INTERESTED IN SORCELINE?
WHY? WHAT DO YOU WANT FROM HER?
NOTHING! NOTHING! UH . . . IT'S ALL GOOD!
OH . . . OK. THEN YOU DON'T NEED TO WORRY ABOUT ME.

Pixie (tiny fairy)
Latin name: Filolae

Habitat:
mountains,
forests, plains

Height: 4 inches

Pixies are small fairies that fly around, cast spells, and influence the future. They can also bestow special powers on newborns.

Strictly diurnal, they are inactive after sundown.

SO, THEIR PRESENCE IS UNUSUAL . . .

BALZAR IS RIGHT! PIXIES DON'T COME OUT AT NIGHT.

PRETTY WEIRD!

YEAH, REALLY BIZARRE!

THEY MUST BE SICK OR SOMETHING TO BE WANDERING AROUND AT NIGHT . . .

MAYBE THEY AREN'T SICK, BUT HAVE SOMETHING TO DO WITH TARA'S DISAPPEARANCE.

EITHER WAY, WE HAVE TO FIGURE OUT WHAT'S WRONG WITH THEM.

OR WHAT THEY'RE UP TO . . .

IT COULD BE A REALLY GOOD SUBJECT FOR OUR FINAL PAPER.

YES, AND AN INTERESTING CASE TO INVESTIGATE!

The next morning . . .

NO, STILL NO SIGN OF TARA.

"SOB"

I'M NOT GOING TO CONTACT HER FAMILY JUST YET, AND WE'RE NOT GOING TO PANIC AND SEND YOU ALL HOME.

PHEW!

IN THE MEANTIME, WE HAVE WORK TO DO!

WE NEED TO PREPARE THE GORGON'S UNICORN BLOOD CURE.

ALCIDE, COME WITH US TONIGHT, WE'RE—

OK!

UH, HANG ON, I DIDN'T EVEN TELL YOU WHERE WE'RE GOING . . .

HA! HE'D FOLLOW YOU TO THE ENDS OF THE EARTH . . .

CAN ANYONE TELL ME WHAT THIS LIQUID IS?

IT'S A LIQUID BIOFUGE! YOU CAN USE IT TO SEE WHETHER A SUBSTANCE IS LIVING OR NOT.

YES, VERY GOOD. YOU SEE, IF I DROP A STONE INTO IT . . .

NOTHING HAPPENS!

BUT IF I DROP SOME UNICORN BLOOD IN THE VIAL . . .

IT REJECTS IT. IT DOESN'T LIKE LIVING THINGS.

glug glug glug

WILLA! I DIDN'T TELL YOU TO START!

IT ISN'T UNICORN BLOOD, PROFESSOR . . .

I SEE THAT! ONLY HUMAN ELEMENTS CAN PROVOKE THIS SORT OF REACTION . . .

BUT I ONLY DROPPED A SHARD OF GLASS IN IT.

ONE FROM THE PLACE WHERE TARA DISAPPEARED!

YOU DID WHAT?!

OH, COME ON! PLAYING AROUND WHILE ONE OF US IS MISSING? HAVE YOU NO SHAME?!

SHE COULD BE DEAD! AND NONE OF YOU SEEM TO CARE! ESPECIALLY YOU TWO!

PFFF! SO NOT TRUE! DON'T LISTEN TO HER.

BUZZ OFF, ARLENE!

HEY, CALM DOWN!

EVERYONE SEEMS TO BE A BIT UPTIGHT THIS MORNING! I'M GOING TO LEAVE YOU TO YOUR OWN DEVICES FOR THE REST OF THE DAY. I'LL CONCENTRATE ON FINDING TARA . . .

ARLENE! DO YOU WANNA EAT?

YOU SHOULD HAVE COME WITH US, WE HAD A GREAT DAY!

YEAH, WELL, IT WOULDN'T HAVE BEEN SO GREAT IF SHE'D BEEN THERE . . .

SORCELINE! LOOK! MORE PIXIES!

ALCIDE! COME ON!

BECAUSE THEY'RE PROBABLY RESPONSIBLE FOR TARA'S DISAPPEARANCE. WE CAN'T LET THEM GET AWAY!

WE'VE SEEN SO MANY CREATURES TODAY. WHY DO WE HAVE TO RUN AFTER SOME FAIRIES?

IT'S REALLY MORE LIKELY THAT THEY HAVE SOME STRANGE ILLNESS. WE SHOULD FIGURE OUT WHAT'S WRONG WITH THEM.

WHAT ARE YOU GUYS TALKING ABOUT?

SO, WHERE'D THE PIXIES GO?

THEY DISAPPEARED! YOU SCARED THEM OFF WITH YOUR CONSTANT WHINING.

HOW STRANGE. I FEEL THEIR PRESENCE BUT CAN'T SEE THEM!

WE NEED TO GET BACK. IT'S ALMOST . . .

11 O'CLOCK!!!

WE'VE BEEN LOOKING FOR YOU EVERYWHERE, FOR HOURS!

WHERE HAVE YOU KIDS BEEN? WE WERE WORRIED SICK ABOUT YOU!

DON'T YOU UNDERSTAND? I THOUGHT THAT ALL OF YOU BUT MERODE HAD DISAPPEARED!

AND WHAT'S THIS . . . "COUGH COUGH COUGH"

TAKE IT EASY, ARCHIBALD.

HRMPH . . . SO WHAT WERE THE FOUR OF YOU UP TO?!

FOUR?

DON'T TELL ME . . .

And that's when we realized that Arlene had disappeared . . .

The Isle of Vorn is even creepier—and more awesome—than I thought.

But this new disappearance is really worrying Willa.

NOOOOOOO!

YOU SEE THESE? THE SAME GLASS SHARDS THAT WERE IN THE SPOT WHERE TARA DISAPPEARED.

I WONDER IF ARLENE WAS HERE WHEN WE CAME BY BEFORE!

THAT WAS JUST BEFORE WE SAW THE PIXIES. THEY ALWAYS SEEM TO BE THERE WHEN SOMEONE DISAPPEARS!

I really don't think they're involved, Willa . . .

MAYBE . . . BUT THERE'S SOMETHING SUSPICIOUS ABOUT THEM. WHY DID THEY DISAPPEAR WHEN WE WENT LOOKING FOR THEM IN THE FIELD OF FLOWERS?

The flowers! That's it!

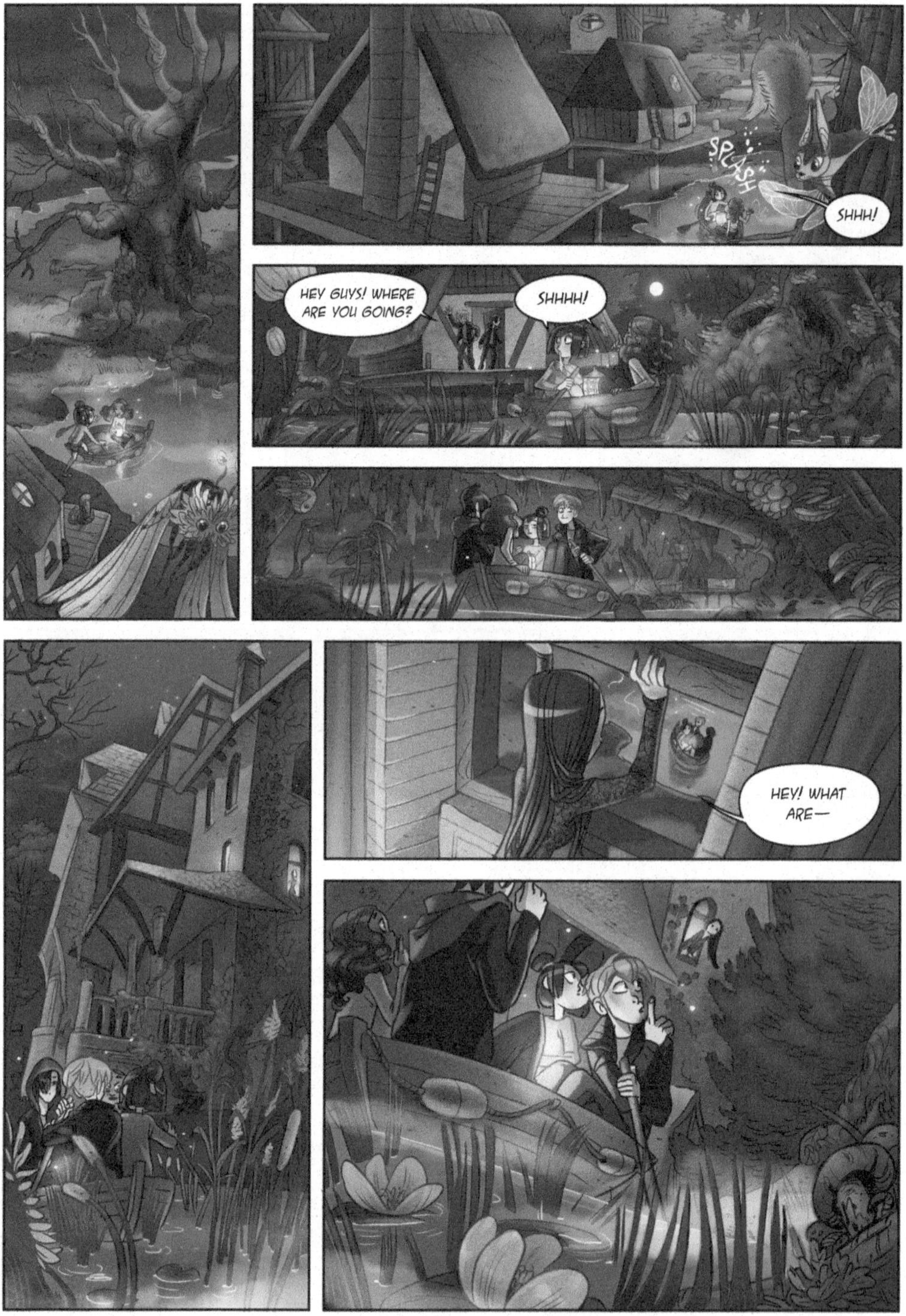

SPLASH
SHHH!
HEY GUYS! WHERE ARE YOU GOING?
SHHHH!
HEY! WHAT ARE—

ALL RIGHT, WHY ARE WE HERE, SORCELINE?

LOOK!

THE FIELD OF "FLOWERS" IS IN FACT . . .

A FIELD OF PIXIES!

FOR SOME STRANGE REASON, THE ZOMBIE PIXIES CLING ONTO THESE BLADES OF GRASS . . .

AND THEY JUST STAY THERE, IMMOBILE, FOR WHO KNOWS HOW LONG . . .

OW!
STUPID FAIRY!

I'LL GET HER FOR YOU!

FORGET IT, MERODE! IT DOESN'T MATTER.

THIS IS YOUR GREAT DISCOVERY?! I THOUGHT YOU WERE GOING TO MAKE A LINK TO TARA AND ARLENE'S DISAPPEARANCES!

I ALREADY TOLD YOU! I DON'T THINK THE PIXIES ARE CONNECTED TO THE DISAPPEARANCES.

THESE CREATURES ARE SICK. WE NEED TO FIGURE OUT WHAT THEY HAVE SO WE CAN CURE THEM.

SHE'S RIGHT! WE'RE HERE TO TREAT SICK CREATURES . . .

ARGGH!

AND WE CAN'T JUST WAVE A MAGIC WAND TO HEAL THEM. IT TAKES TIME!

EXACTLY.

?

I DIDN'T WANT TO COME! THEY MADE ME COME WITH THEM!

MADAME S. TOLD YOU, DIDN'T SHE? THE VAMPIRE LADY.

HOW DO YOU KNOW SHE'S A VAMPIRE?

PROFESSOR BALZAR? WHAT ARE YOU DOING HERE?

SORCELINE NOTICED.

HMM! INTERESTING.

COME QUICK! IT'S UNBELIEVABLE! HURRY!

I RAN TO FIND YOU WHEN I SAW THIS PETRIFIED PIXIE. MERODE STAYED BACK WITH HER.

I JUST . . . FOUND HER . . .

TARA AND ARLENE WERE TURNED TO GLASS . . .

WHOEVER DID IT SMASHED THE STATUES BEFORE WE COULD FIND THEM . . .

BUT TONIGHT, THERE WASN'T TIME TO DESTROY THE EVIDENCE . . .

YOU MEAN, MADAME S. DIDN'T HAVE TIME . . .

HUH?

YOU HAVEN'T FIGURED OUT THAT MADAME S. IS THE CULPRIT?

SORCELINE, CAN I SPEAK TO YOU FOR A MOMENT?

WILL YOU TELL ME MORE ABOUT MADAME S.?

UH . . . YOU MEAN ABOUT THE FACT THAT SHE'S GUILTY?

HA! HA! HA! WHAT AN IMAGINATION!

NO! I WANT TO KNOW HOW YOU FIGURED OUT SHE WAS A VAMPIRE!

NO IDEA! INTUITION! A SIXTH SENSE . . .

YOU WERE ADOPTED, RIGHT?

SO?

AND THEN HE JUST CHANGED THE SUBJECT . . .

HE SAID MY THEORY ABOUT THE PIXIES WAS INTERESTING.

HE ENCOURAGED ME TO RESEARCH IT FURTHER. IT'S A GOOD TOPIC FOR A CRYPTOZOOLOGIST.

AH, I SEE WE'RE GOING TO GET BORING NOW!

SHHHH! I'D REALLY LIKE TO GET SOME SLEEP!

WELL, GO BACK TO YOUR HUT THEN . . .

YOU KNOW IT'S NOT SAFE. THAT'S WHY WE SHOULD ALL STAY HERE TOGETHER.

YEAH! AND AS CLOSE TO SORCELINE AS POSSIBLE!

!!!

I CAN'T SLEEP EITHER. I'M GOING TO CHECK ON THE GORGON.

WAIT! I'M COMING WITH YOU . . .

WHAT'S SHE DOING HERE?

GOOD QUESTION!

HEY, I'VE FOUND IT!

HMM?

LOOK! DO YOU REMEMBER THE CALADRIUS IN THE FIELD OF FLOWERS WHERE THE PIXIES WERE?

Flos caladrio: Flower that attracts the caladrius

THESE FLOWER PETALS LOOK EXACTLY LIKE THE PIXIES' WINGS!

SO?

SOMETHING IS ATTACKING THE FAIRIES' BRAINS AND TURNING THEM INTO ZOMBIES!

THE HYPNOTIZED PIXIES CLIMB UP THE BLADES OF GRASS AND CLAMP ON; THEY WAIT FOR HOURS FOR A CALADRIUS TO COME AND EAT THEM.

WHAT DOES IT ALL MEAN? DO THE CALADRIUSES HAVE SPECIAL POWERS OVER THE PIXIES?

CAN'T WE THINK ABOUT IT TOMORROW?

PERK UP, EVERYONE!

I KNOW WE'VE ALL BEEN MISSING SLEEP LATELY, BUT WE CAN'T NEGLECT THE CREATURES . . .

THE CALADRIUS EGGS ARE GOING TO HATCH AND WE NEED TO BE THERE TO TAKE CARE OF THE CHICKS!

LIKE I SAID, MERODE AND I SAW IT. WE DIDN'T BOTH IMAGINE IT, YOU KNOW!

IMPOSSIBLE.

MADAME S. WAS JUST BLOODLETTING THE GORGON. THAT'S ALL.

WHAT?

BLOODLETTING . . . IT'S THE ANCIENT PRACTICE OF DRAWING BLOOD FROM A PATIENT TO HELP CURE THEM.

CHEEP CHEEP!

SHE WAS BLOODLETTING, I'LL GIVE YOU THAT . . .

BUT SHE DRANK THE BLOOD HERSELF TO INCREASE HER POWER!

THAT'S HOW SHE'S ABLE TO PETRIFY HER VICTIMS WITH ONE GLANCE.

AND SINCE THE GORGON'S POWER HAS WEAKENED, SHE DOESN'T TURN HER VICTIMS TO STONE—BUT TO GLASS!

EXACTLY! THAT'S IT! THAT FITS, DON'T YOU THINK?

NAH.

WHAT'S MADAME S.'S MOTIVE?

?

KRKLE

Everyone is wondering why a serpent hatched from the caladrius egg. It's really strange.

But I just realized something even more frightening . . .

CURSE TARA!

BUZZ OFF, ARLENE!

OW! STUPID FAIRY!

Everyone who's been turned to glass was cursed . . .

. . . BY ME.

39

WHERE HAVE YOU BEEN? I'VE BEEN LOOKING EVERYWHERE FOR YOU . . .

If I'm the cause of the disappearances, am I even human? Could I possibly be a cryptid?

Willa is persistent; she'll eventually figure out that it's all my fault.

It's not easy to investigate with your best friend when you're the guilty one . . .

I have to distract her.

WE NEED TO FOLLOW MADAME S.

HELP ME FIGURE OUT THE MYSTERY OF THE PIXIES FIRST. PLEASE?

I FOUND WHAT KIND OF SNAKE IT IS!

THEY CAN'T REPRODUCE. THERE ARE ONLY MALES AND NO FEMALES.

YOU KNOW WHAT THAT MEANS, RIGHT?

THEY'RE ALL MACHO AND SEXIST.

HA! HA! HA!

NO! IT MEANS THEY'VE FOUND ANOTHER WAY TO REPRODUCE— LIKE PARASITISM, FOR EXAMPLE.

COME ON! WE'RE GOING TO VERIFY THIS!

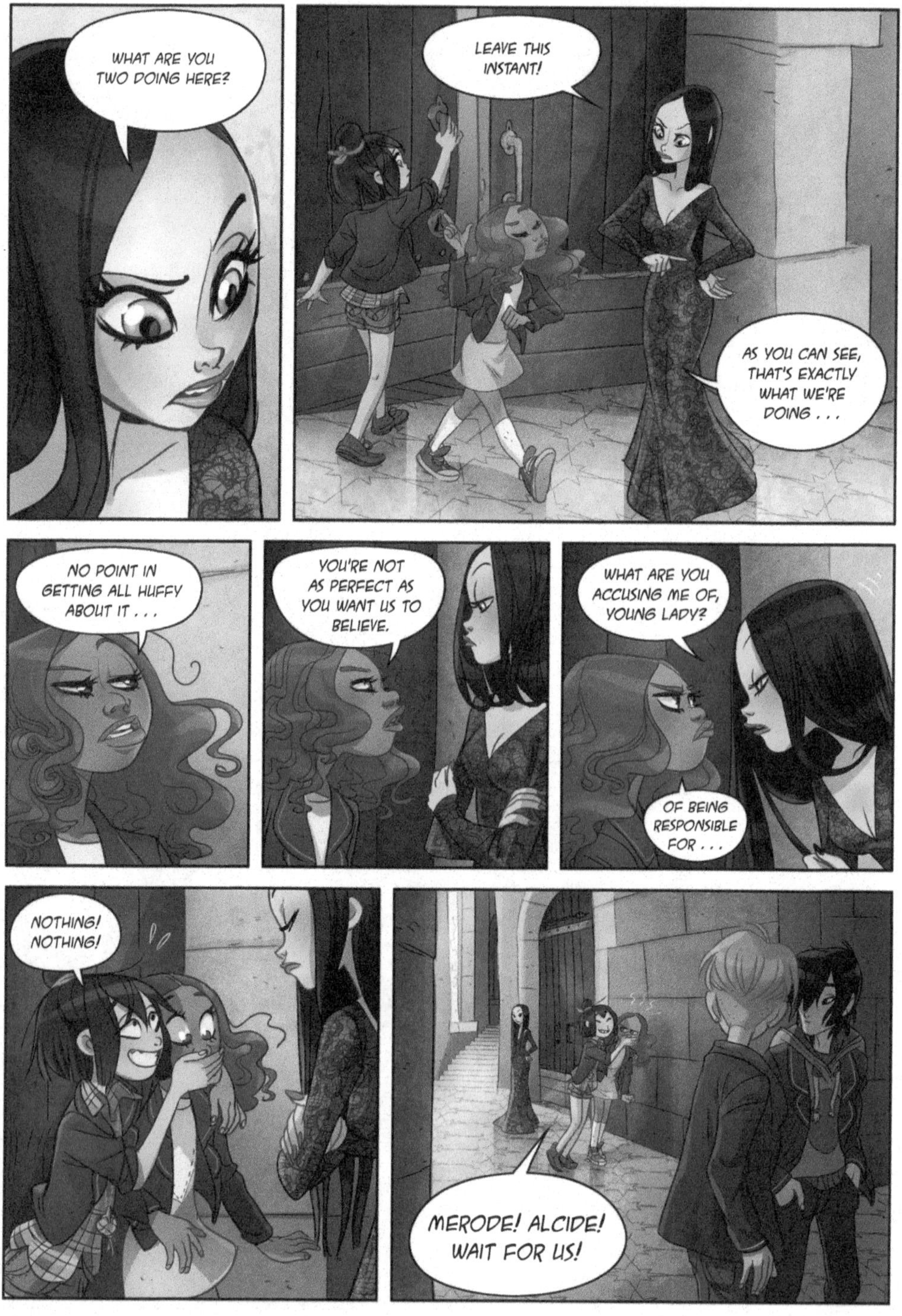
WHAT ARE YOU TWO DOING HERE?
LEAVE THIS INSTANT!
AS YOU CAN SEE, THAT'S EXACTLY WHAT WE'RE DOING . . .
NO POINT IN GETTING ALL HUFFY ABOUT IT . . .
YOU'RE NOT AS PERFECT AS YOU WANT US TO BELIEVE.
WHAT ARE YOU ACCUSING ME OF, YOUNG LADY?
OF BEING RESPONSIBLE FOR . . .
NOTHING! NOTHING!
MERODE! ALCIDE! WAIT FOR US!

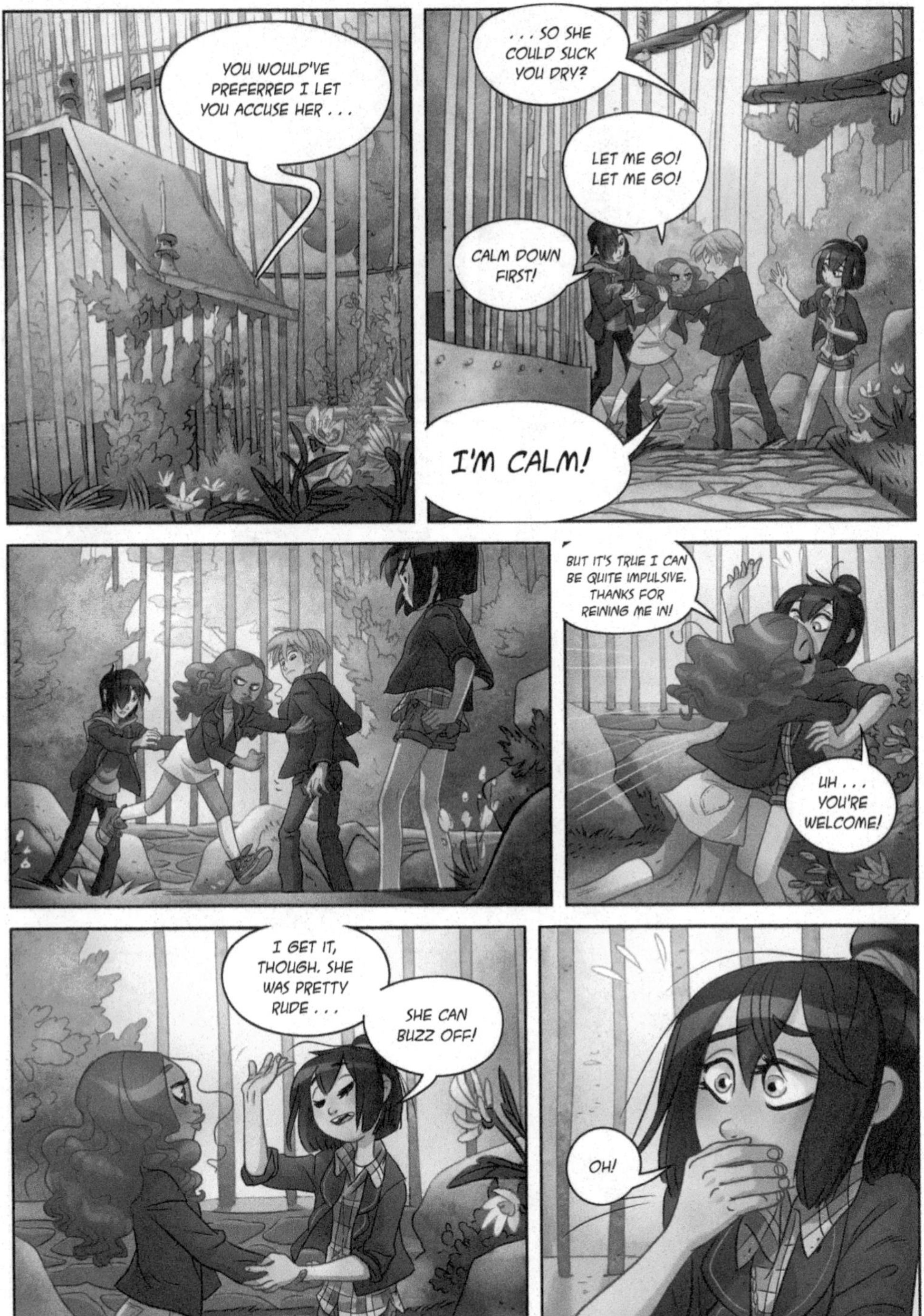
YOU WOULD'VE PREFERRED I LET YOU ACCUSE HER . . .
. . . SO SHE COULD SUCK YOU DRY?
LET ME GO! LET ME GO!
CALM DOWN FIRST!
I'M CALM!
BUT IT'S TRUE I CAN BE QUITE IMPULSIVE. THANKS FOR REINING ME IN!
UH . . . YOU'RE WELCOME!
I GET IT, THOUGH. SHE WAS PRETTY RUDE . . .
SHE CAN BUZZ OFF!
OH!

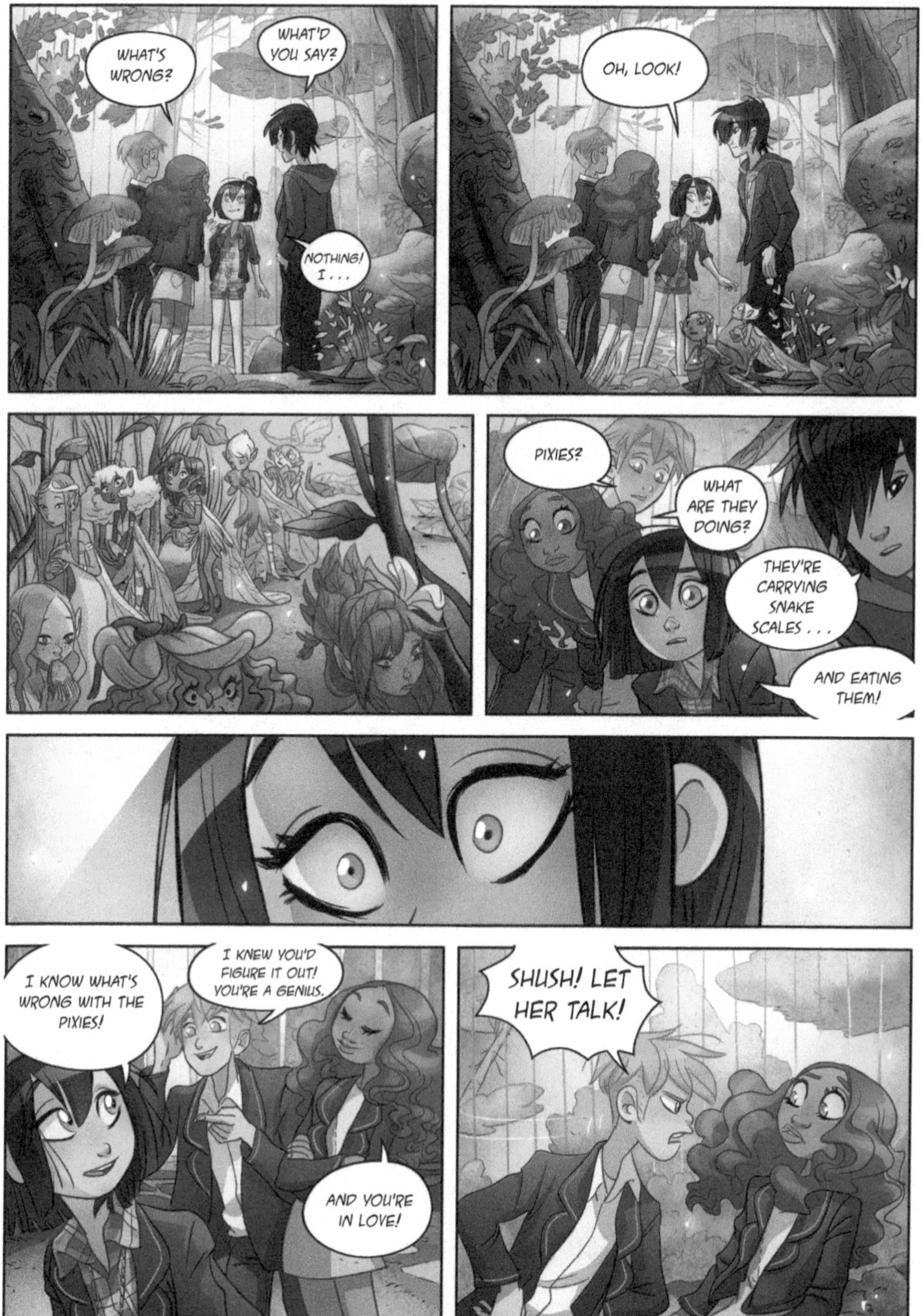
WHAT'S WRONG?
WHAT'D YOU SAY?
NOTHING! I . . .
OH, LOOK!
PIXIES?
WHAT ARE THEY DOING?
THEY'RE CARRYING SNAKE SCALES . . .
AND EATING THEM!
I KNOW WHAT'S WRONG WITH THE PIXIES!
I KNEW YOU'D FIGURE IT OUT! YOU'RE A GENIUS.
AND YOU'RE IN LOVE!
SHUSH! LET HER TALK!

ONE OF NATURE'S GREATEST MYSTERIES IS, WITHOUT A DOUBT, THE CYCLE OF THE LIVER FLUKE. YOU COULD WRITE VOLUMES ON THAT CREATURE, AND PEOPLE HAVE . . .

THE LIVER FLUKE IS A PARASITE THAT LIVES IN THE LIVERS OF SHEEP. IT LAYS EGGS THERE, BUT THE EGGS CAN'T HATCH . . .

. . . So they pass through the sheep's digestive tract. Once out, they can hatch and make larvae.

If a snail, for example, encounters the sheep's excrement, it becomes infected.

The larvae multiply inside the snail, and then get spat out.

Then some ants, attracted by the pearls that form in the snail's spit, swallow the fluke.

But the fluke ultimately needs to return to the sheep's liver in order to reproduce. So it takes over the brains of the ants . . .

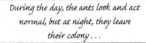

During the day, the ants look and act normal, but at night, they leave their colony . . .

And cling to the tips of tall grasses.

But not just any grasses— the ones the sheep like to eat!

JUST LIKE THE PIXIES!

REMARKABLE! WELL DONE!

SO, JUST AS THE ANTS EAT THE INFECTED SNAIL SPIT, THE PIXIES HAVE BEEN EATING INFECTED SNAKE SCALES . . .

THE PARASITE IS FORCING THEM TO PERCH ON TOP OF BLADES OF GRASS . . .

. . . AND SPREAD THEIR WINGS, MAKING THEM LOOK LIKE . . .

. . . the flowers that attract the caladrius.

AND WHEN THE CALADRIUS IS INFECTED, THE PARASITE DEVELOPS IN ITS EGGS . . .

SO THE EGGS DON'T HATCH CHICKS, BUT SNAKES!

YOU ARE AN EXCEPTIONAL STUDENT! I MEAN . . . AN EXTRAORDINARY BEING!

JUST HOW EXTRAORDINARY?

I . . . IT'S . . . IT'S NOT ME YOU SHOULD ASK!

MOM?

HELLO DEAR, YOU OK?

IT'S NICE OF YOU TO CALL. WHAT IS IT?

HOW ARE THE CLASSES? HAVE YOU MADE FRIENDS?

OH, I MISS YOU! I CAN'T WAIT . . .

MOM, WAS I ADOPTED?

?

46

PROFESSOR BALZAR MUST HAVE DOCUMENTS ABOUT ME HIDDEN IN HIS OFFICE.

DON'T WORRY... WE'LL FIND THEM IN NO TIME...

I'VE ALMOST GOT IT!

THERE!

I HEAR SOMETHING!

IF THERE WERE SOMEONE IN THERE, THEY WOULD ALREADY HAVE OPENED THE DOOR.

"CLICK"

WHO... WHO'S THERE?

WE'RE BUSTED... I KNEW IT!

ARE YOU IN SHAPE FOR A 100 METER DASH?

AAAAHHH!

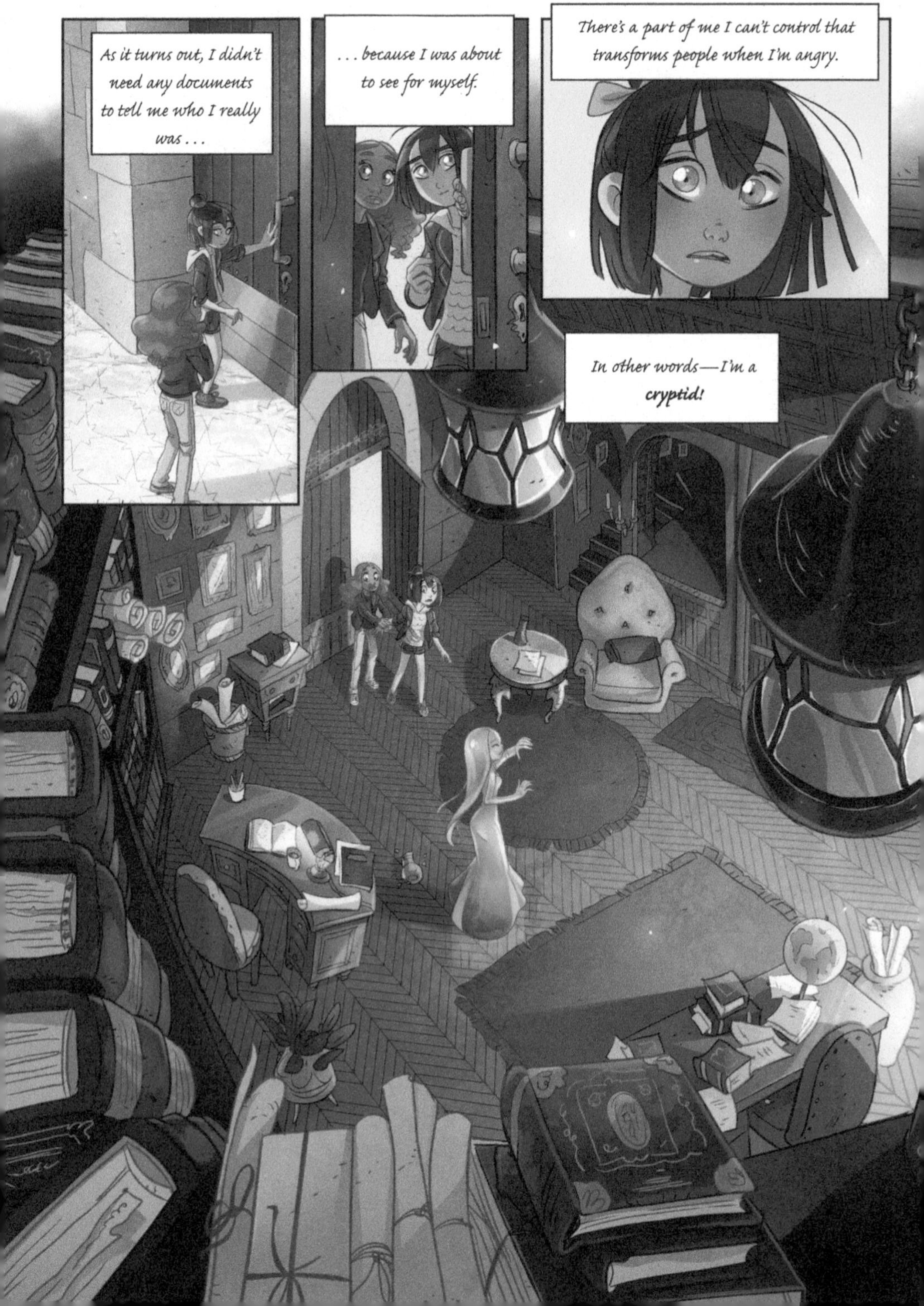

As it turns out, I didn't need any documents to tell me who I really was . . .
. . . because I was about to see for myself.
There's a part of me I can't control that transforms people when I'm angry.
In other words—I'm a **cryptid!**

Part 2

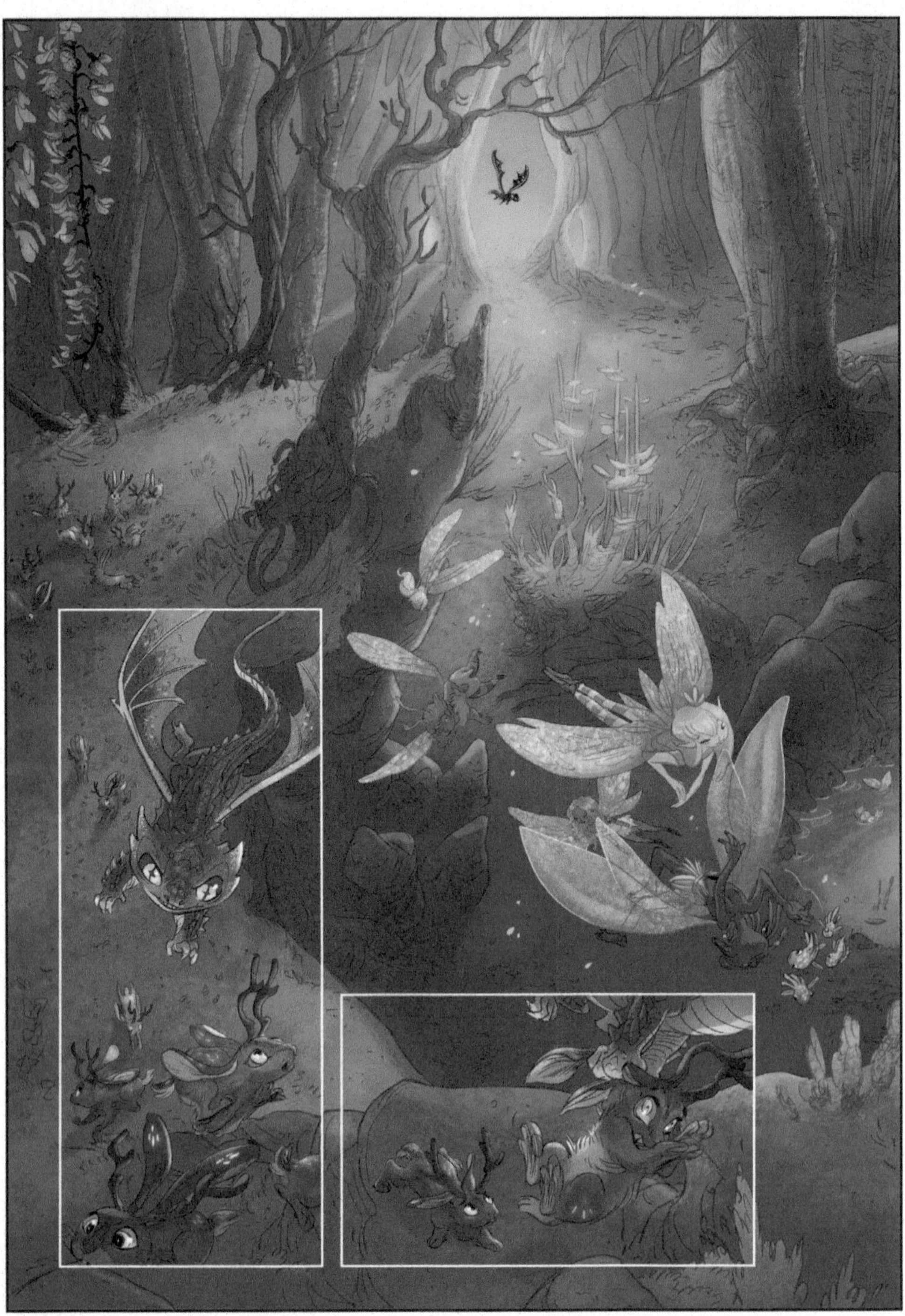

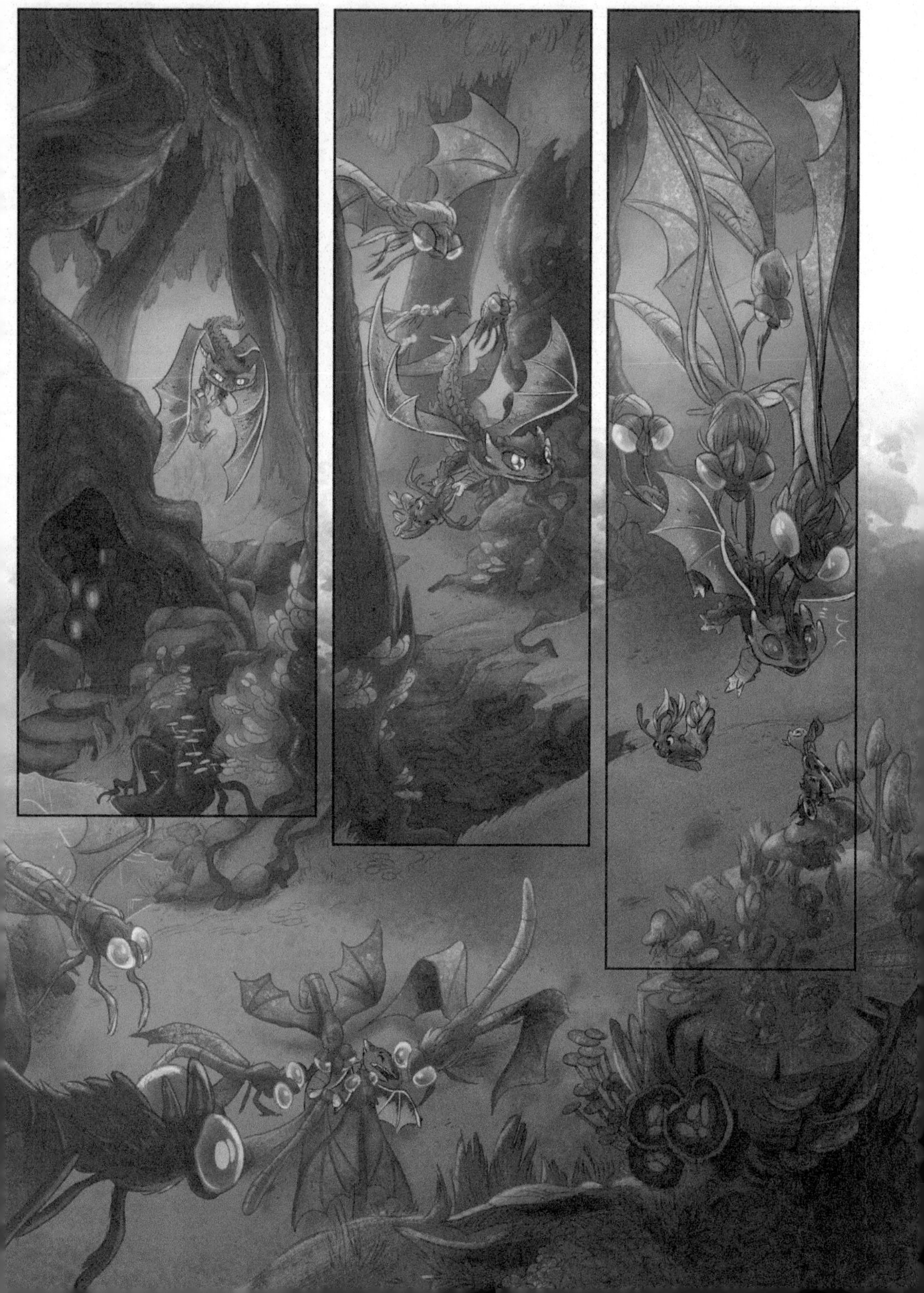

Dear Mom, I arrived safely on Vorn. My vacation has been fun so far . . .

This is the group.

Unfortunately, one night while we were out on an excursion, Tara was turned into a glass statue. She was the first victim in a series of attacks.

The same thing happened to another girl, Arlene; then to Madame S.; and finally, to an adorable little pixie!

Don't worry, this won't happen to me because . . . well, because I'm the one doing it!

It's horrible! I have the power to turn people to glass when I get angry! I have no idea how or why! Mom, do you know anything about this?

SORCELINE! YOU WITH US?

UH . . . COULD YOU REPEAT THE QUESTION, PLEASE?

HMM!

I UNDERSTAND THAT THE RECENT EVENTS HAVE SHAKEN US ALL . . . BUT WE MUST NOT FORGET THE ANIMALS IN OUR CARE. THEY NEED US!

WOULD SOMEONE REPEAT WHAT I SAID FOR SORCELINE?

YES, ME!

PFFF, BIG SURPRISE!

THESE MERMAIDS HAVE VERRUCULA EMINET SUBLIMIS . . .

THAT IS, MIGRATING SORES . . .

THESE SORES DON'T STAY IN THE SAME PLACE . . . BUT CONTINUALLY MOVE AROUND TO DIFFERENT PLACES ON THE BODY.

VERY GOOD, ALCIDE.

I'D MUCH RATHER HAVE AN AVERAGE BUT ATTENTIVE ASSISTANT THAN A LAZY BUT BRILLIANT ONE . . .

ME? AVERAGE?

THIS TYPE OF SORE IS VERY DIFFICULT TO HEAL. AS SOON AS YOU TRY AND DISINFECT IT—SWISH—IT MOVES!

ALCIDE ISN'T REALLY THE COMPETITION.

YOU'RE WRONG. EVERYONE IS THE COMPETITION. AND THE BEST ONE WILL WIN!

HEALING VERRUCULA EMINET SUBLIMIS IS LIKE CATCHING A MOUSE. YOU HAVE TO PUT BARRIERS IN ITS WAY!

YES, BUT IF ALCIDE DOES GET TOO FAR AHEAD . . .

ALL YOU HAVE TO DO IS TURN HIM INTO GLASS!

?

JUST RUB THE MERMAID'S SKIN WITH STINGING NETTLE. THAT WILL CAUSE BLISTERS TO FORM OVER THE SORES.

THE BLISTERS WILL STOP THE SORES FROM MOVING, AND THEN YOU CAN HEAL THEM.

WHAT? WHAT'S WRONG? WHAT DID HE SAY TO SORCELINE?

LET HER GO! CAN'T YOU SEE YOU'RE SUFFOCATING HER?

ME? I'M SUFFOCATING SORCELINE? WHAT ABOUT MERODE? HE'S NOT ANY BETTER! I'LL HAVE YOU KNOW, HE THREATENED ME!

HUH? WHAT?

PROMISE YOU WON'T SAY ANYTHING?

NOOOOO . . .

YEEESSS!

MERODE IS PLAYING THE STRONG SILENT TYPE, BUT HE ACTUALLY REALLY LIKES YOU.

THAT'S WHY HE KNOWS SO MUCH ABOUT ME . . .

I'M GONNA KEEP A CLOSER EYE ON HIM.

CAN YOU TELL ME EXACTLY WHAT ALCIDE TOLD YOU?

ONE NIGHT, ALCIDE ASKED MERODE WHAT HE THOUGHT OF YOU, AND SUDDENLY . . .

MERODE GRABBED HIM BY THE THROAT . . .

AND YELLED . . .

"WHY?! WHAT DO YOU WANT FROM SORCELINE?!"

56

I THOUGHT SHE WAS ATTACKING YOU . . .

OWW!! HEY!

STAY AWAY FROM US IF YOU VALUE YOUR LIFE!

THIS IS DISGUSTING!

YUCK!

HERE! TAKE MINE! IT'LL MAKE YOU FORGET YOUR HEADACHE!

WHAT IS IT?

HEY! HELLO! I'M THE ONE WHO ASKED THE QUESTION, NOT YOUR PHONE!

SORRY! I'M TRYING TO REACH MY MOM BUT SHE'S NOT ANSWERING.

IT'S LIKE SHE'S AVOIDING ME.

MMM . . . THIS IS GOOD! WHAT IS IT?

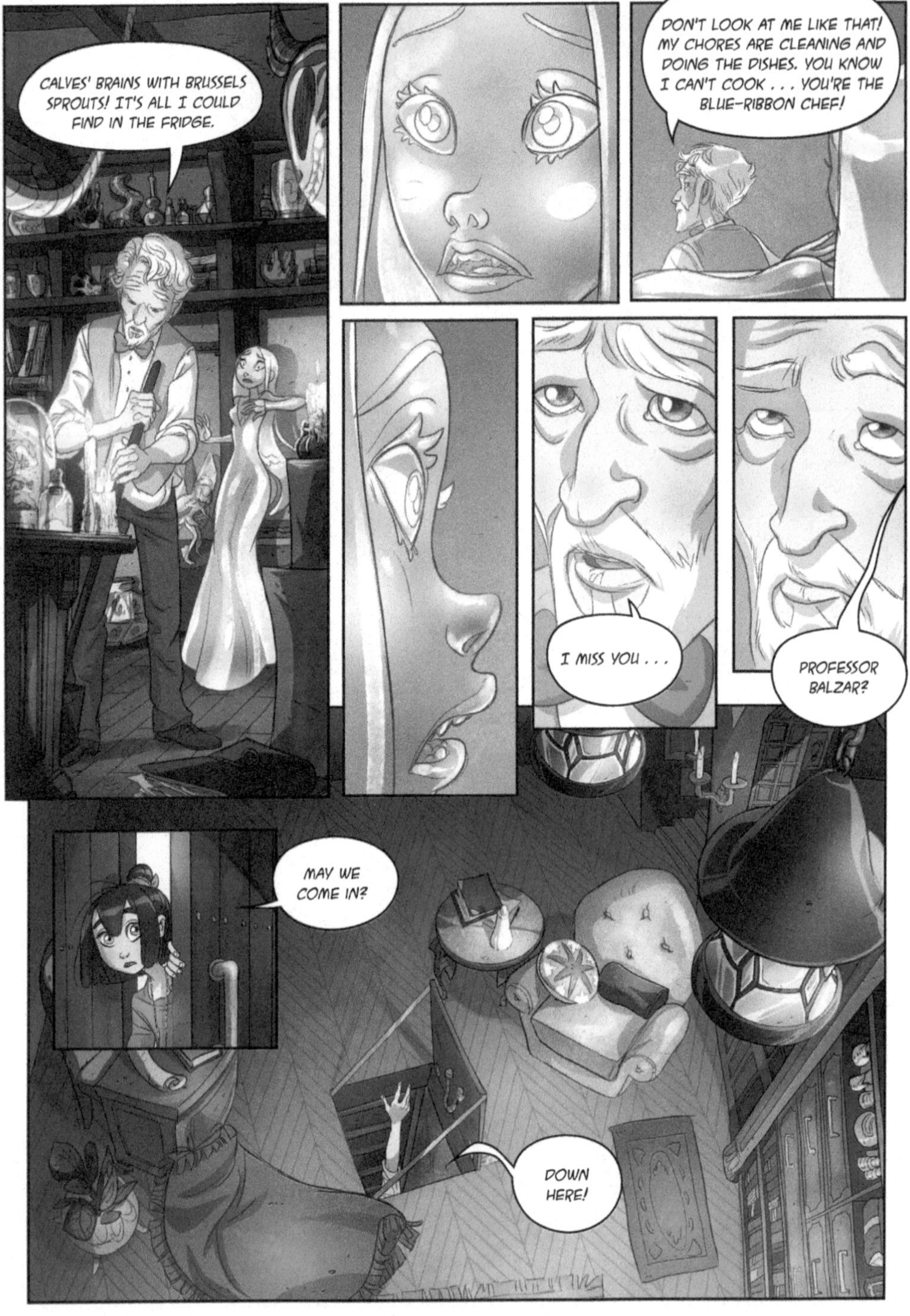
CALVES' BRAINS WITH BRUSSELS SPROUTS! IT'S ALL I COULD FIND IN THE FRIDGE.
DON'T LOOK AT ME LIKE THAT! MY CHORES ARE CLEANING AND DOING THE DISHES. YOU KNOW I CAN'T COOK . . . YOU'RE THE BLUE-RIBBON CHEF!
I MISS YOU . . .
PROFESSOR BALZAR?
MAY WE COME IN?
DOWN HERE!

Wow! I wish my bedroom back home looked like this...

WHERE WOULD YOU PUT YOUR BED?

WHO'D NEED ONE? NO TIME FOR SLEEP IN SUCH A PLACE!

WILL YOU INVITE ME TO YOUR ROOM OF WONDERS?

SURE, BUT YOU'LL HAVE TO FORCE ME TO LEAVE THIS ONE FIRST!

I'VE CALLED US TOGETHER THIS AFTERNOON TO DISCUSS THE MYSTERY THAT CONCERNS US ALL.

OUR FRIENDS WHO HAVE BEEN TURNED TO GLASS ARE ALL HERE. IN-TACT OR IN PIECES.

WHERE'S ALCIDE?

FAR AWAY FROM ME—THAT'S ALL THAT MATTERS!

I THINK HE WANTED TO DO HIS HOMEWORK.

EXCELLENT, GOOD FOR HIM. LET'S GET STARTED.

PERSONALLY, I THINK THE GORGON HAS SOMETHING TO DO WITH WHAT'S GOING ON...

THAT'S WHAT I THINK TOO, WILLA.

MERODE! YOU'RE THE ONE WHO'S HEALING THE GORGON. DO YOU THINK SHE'S STRONG ENOUGH TO BE PETRIFYING PEOPLE?

ACTUALLY, I HAVE MY OWN THEORY...

Argh!

!!!

59

He's going to tell them it's me! Say something, Sorceline! Anything!

ABOUT MADAME S.? BECAUSE OF THE NIGHT WE SAW HER DRINKING THE GORGON'S BLOOD?

WHAT?

Oof! Thanks Willa!

DON'T TELL ME, REALLY? OH, SHE'S STUBBORN!

I WARNED HER THAT THE GORGON COULD BE DANGEROUS.

DID YOU DRINK HER BLOOD TO MAKE HER WEAK?

WERE YOU HOPING THAT WOULD STOP THE ATTACKS?

SADLY, YOU WERE WRONG . . .

WHY ARE YOU SO WORRIED, PROFESSOR? YOU DO KNOW HOW TO TURN EVERYONE BACK, DON'T YOU?

WELL, YES. WHOEVER IS RESPONSIBLE WILL HAVE TO TURN THEMSELVES INTO A STATUE.

SORCELINE!

SINCE YOU'RE SO GOOD AT RECOGNIZING MAGICAL BEINGS . . .

I WANT YOU TO FIND OUT WHICH CREATURE COULD HAVE SUCKED OUT THE GORGON'S MAGIC FLUID.

DON'T WORRY. I WON'T SAY ANYTHING. I JUST WANT TO HELP YOU UNDERSTAND WHAT YOU ARE.

WHY DID YOU TELL SORCELINE WHAT I TOLD YOU ABOUT MERODE? NOW SHE'S INTERESTED IN HIM!

SORCELINE ISN'T INTERESTED IN MERODE BECAUSE SHE'S IN LOVE. SHE'S INTERESTED IN HIM BECAUSE HE'S MYSTERIOUS.

UNLIKE YOU, WHO ARE AS TRANSPARENT AS CAN BE!

!

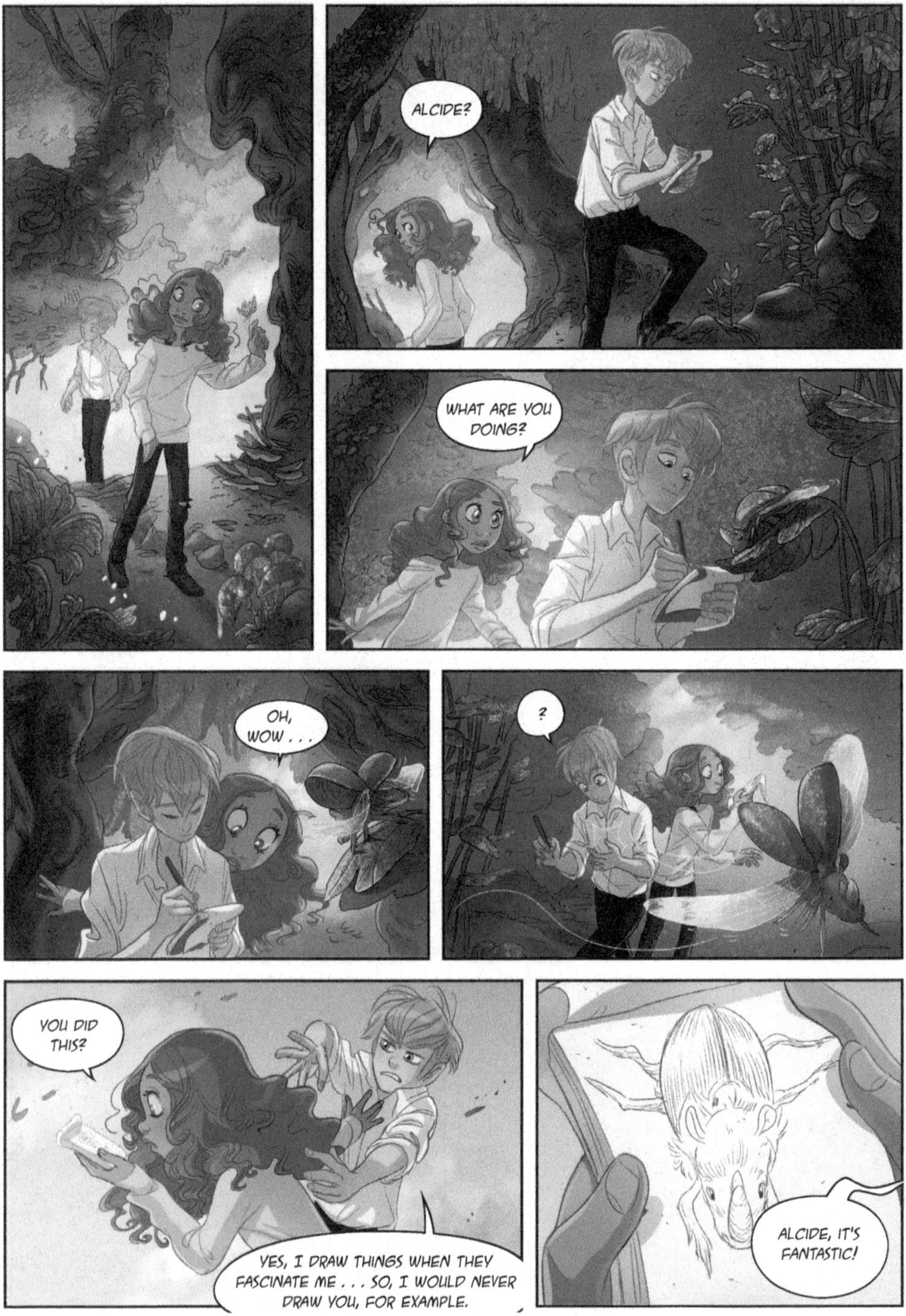
ALCIDE?
WHAT ARE YOU DOING?
OH, WOW . . .
?
YOU DID THIS?
YES, I DRAW THINGS WHEN THEY FASCINATE ME . . . SO, I WOULD NEVER DRAW YOU, FOR EXAMPLE.
ALCIDE, IT'S FANTASTIC!

I WOULD'VE LIKED TO BE A SYLPH. WHEN THEY'RE TAKEN BY SOMEONE . . .

THEY VOW TO PROTECT THAT PERSON. THEY'RE LIKE GUARDIAN ANGELS.

UNLIKE SOME PEOPLE WHO CURSE WHOEVER MAKES THEM ANGRY.

WHAT?

NOTHING, NOTHING . . . IT'S JUST THAT IT'S NICE TO SHARE MY SECRET.

HAVE YOU BEEN DRAWING FOR A LONG TIME?

FOREVER! MY GRANDFATHER WAS AN ENTOMOLOGIST. HE STUDIED BUGS.

I LEARNED HOW TO OBSERVE WILDLIFE FROM HIM WHEN WE TOOK WALKS TOGETHER.

YOU'RE REALLY TALENTED!

IT'S NOT ENOUGH TO HAVE TALENT; YOU HAVE TO LEARN TO BE OBSERVANT.

DO YOU HAVE OTHER DRAWINGS?

YEAH, PLENTY.

I'D LOVE TO SEE THEM.

REALLY?

YEAH!

UH . . . DO YOU THINK SORCELINE WOULD LIKE THEM?

UGH! HERE WE GO AGAIN!

AAAH!

SORCELINE? WHAT'S . . . ?

?

DO WHAT I DO! HURRY!

HA! HA! HA! HA! HA! HA!

I CAN'T BELIEVE IT. ALL YOU HAVE TO DO IS BOW TO THEM!

INCREDIBLE, ISN'T IT?

IT'S WILD!

ESPECIALLY SINCE THE KAPPAS ARE QUITE CUNNING AND DANGEROUS. THEY ATTACK HUMANS EASILY, DRAGGING THEM TO THE BOTTOMS OF LAKES TO EAT THEM.

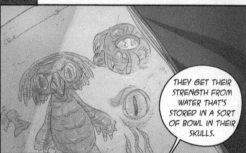

THEY GET THEIR STRENGTH FROM WATER THAT'S STORED IN A SORT OF BOWL IN THEIR SKULLS.

SUCH POLITE CREATURES!

HA! HA! HA! HA! HA!

I HATE TO BE A SPOIL SPORT, BUT WE HAVE A TEST TOMORROW . . .

. . . AND I'D LIKE TO GET SOME SLEEP!

But if you greet them by bowing, they imitate you and the water spills out!

65

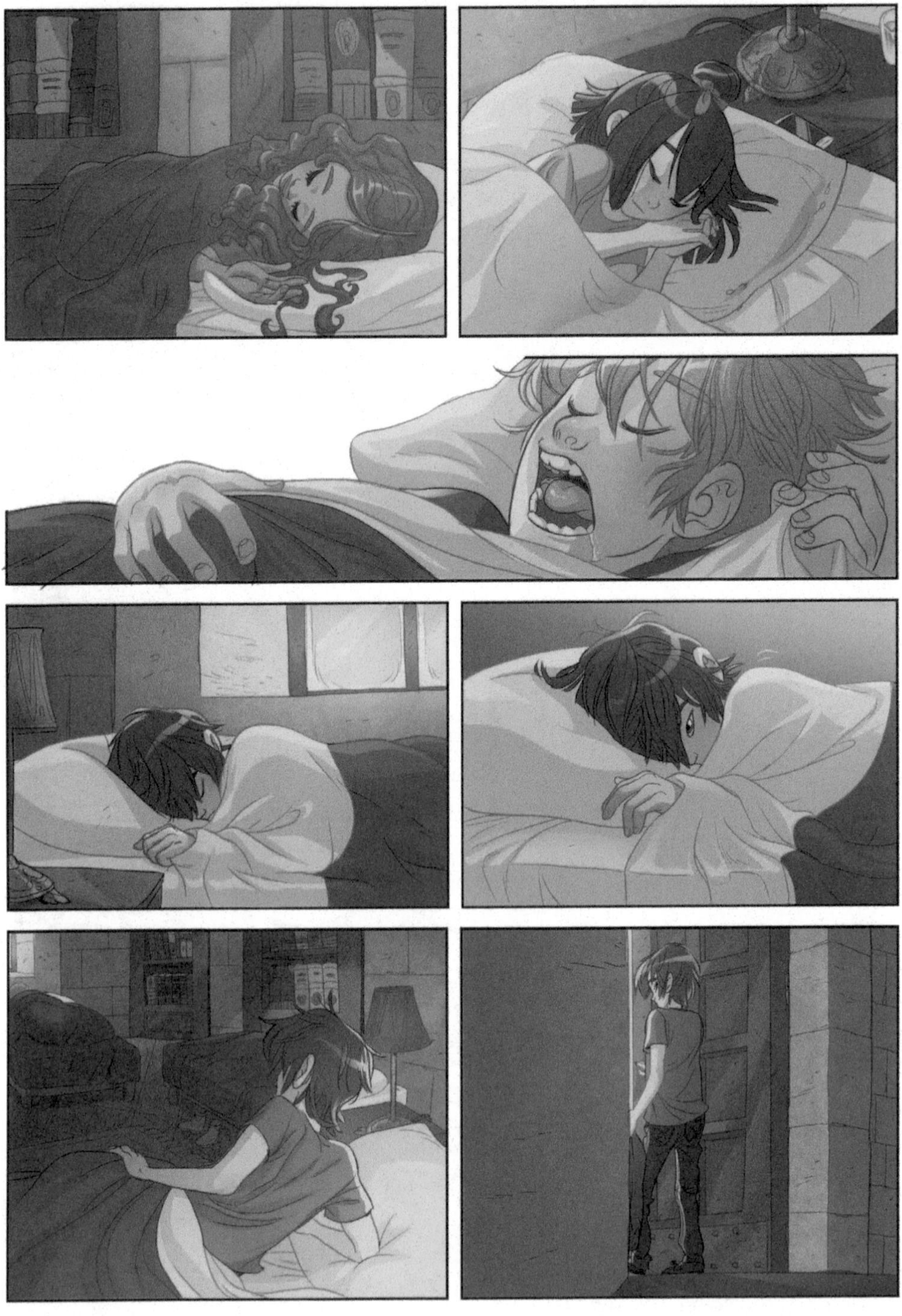

SHHHHHHHHH!

BZZZZZZZZ!

AND SHE DISMISSES ME! UGH!

HOW ARE WE SUPPOSED TO BE SECRET INVESTIGATORS WHEN YOU KEEP BRINGING YOUR PHONE ON MISSIONS?

IT'S A MESSAGE FROM MY MOM! GO ON AHEAD, I'LL CATCH UP.

HI SWEETIE, LISTEN . . . I DON'T KNOW WHO PUT THE ADOPTION NOTION INTO YOUR HEAD. WAS IT YOUR FATHER? DID HE CONTACT YOU?

COME WITH ME, YOUNG LADY!

WHY ARE YOU FOLLOWING ME?

YES, WILLA, I'M TALKING TO YOU!

DID SORCELINE SEND YOU?

WHERE ARE WE GOING, PROFESSOR?

WHERE YOU CAN GET SOME ANSWERS . . .

YOU SEE, SORCELINE, NEITHER I NOR YOUR MOTHER CAN ANSWER YOUR QUESTIONS.

LOOK AROUND, OBSERVE NATURE, AND YOU WILL FIND YOUR WAY!

BUT I DO LOOK AROUND ME, AND I'M SO AMAZED THAT—

FOR NOW, ALL YOU SEE IS THE MAGIC AND THE FAIRIES, BUT YOUR VISION WILL CHANGE.

PROFESSOR, ARE THOSE . . . ?

LUMIOLE EGGS?!

JUDGING BY THEIR COLOR, THEY SHOULD HATCH SOON.

THEY MUST'VE FALLEN FROM THE NEST UP THERE. I'M GOING TO PUT THEM BACK.

WOW!

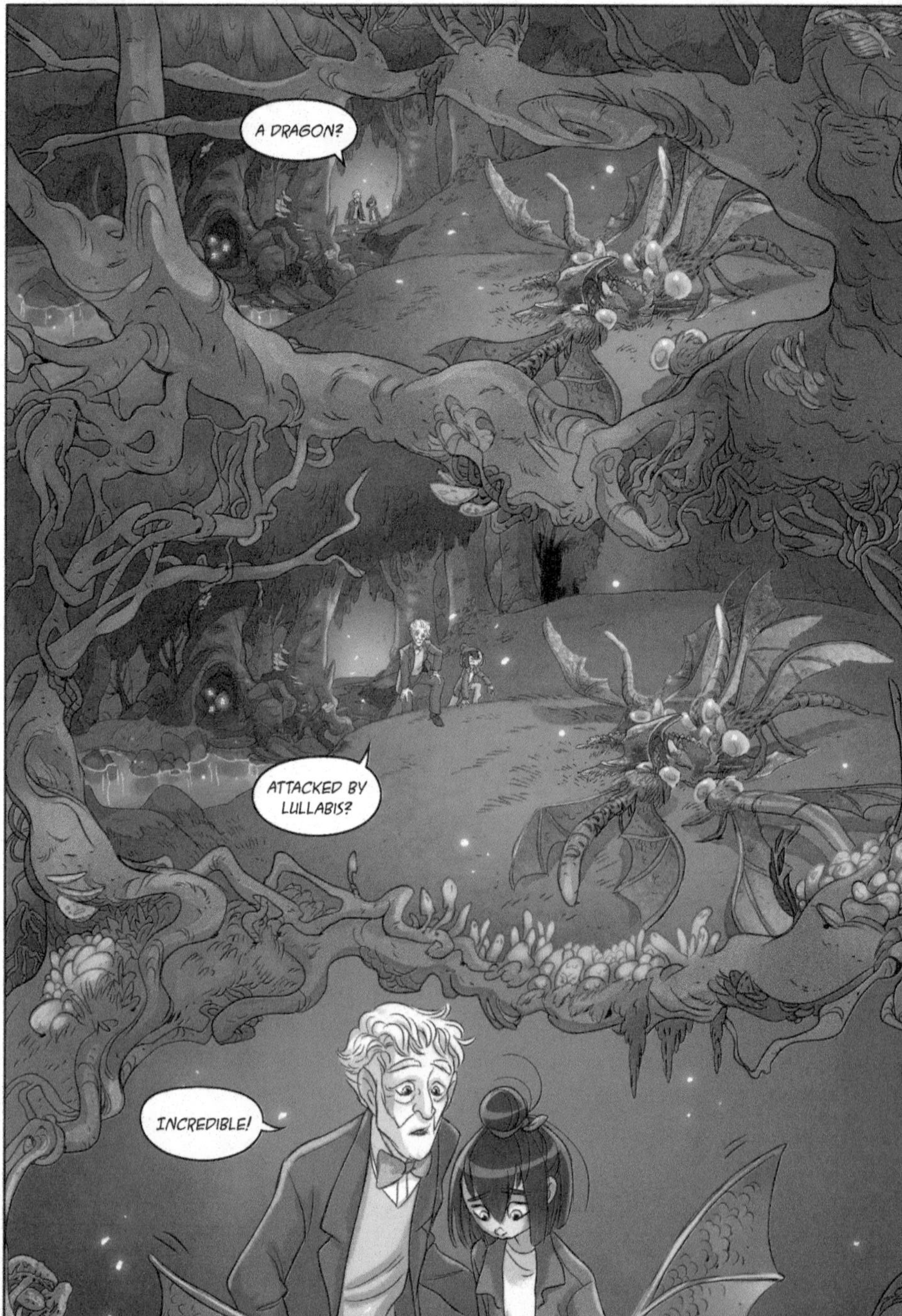
A DRAGON?
ATTACKED BY LULLABIS?
INCREDIBLE!

SORCELINE TOLD YOU ABOUT HER SECRET, RIGHT? THAT'S WHY YOU'RE FOLLOWING ME.

WHAT SECRET?

YOU DON'T KNOW?

UH . . . AH . . . YES, OF COURSE! BUT I FORGOT . . .

HEY, YOUR PATIENT IS GETTING SICKER AND SICKER BY THE DAY! ARE YOU SURE YOU'RE DOING WHAT'S RIGHT FOR HER?

HURRY, PUT IT DOWN HERE!

WILLA! MERODE! PERFECT TIMING! COME AND HELP US!

71

WE FOUND THIS DRAGON IN THE FOREST. LULLABIS WERE SUCKING ITS BLOOD. IT'S STILL CONSCIOUS, BUT IT'S COVERED IN TINY BITES . . .

THAT'S ODD. LULLABIS—

ARE NEVER AGGRESSIVE! THEY'RE HARMLESS, KIND, COMPASSIONATE CREATURES!

THAT'S WHY THEY FOLLOWED YOU ALL RIGHT UP TO THE MANOR WHEN YOU ARRIVED.

RIGHT, SO CAN SOMEONE TELL ME WHAT WE NEED TO DO?

PUT ON FLAME-RETARDANT CLOTHING.

GOOD THOUGHT, WILLA, EXCEPT THAT IT'S A YOUNG DRAGON. TOO YOUNG TO BREATHE FIRE YET.

GOOD ENOUGH, THOUGH, TO EARN YOU THE RIGHT TO TAKE CARE OF IT.

SO, WHAT NEXT?

FIRST, WE NEED TO CHECK AND SEE IF IT HASN'T LOST TOO MUCH BLOOD . . .

PALLOR, COLD SWEATS, THIRST, AND DIZZINESS ARE SIGNS OF SIGNIFICANT BLOOD LOSS.

MERODE, COULD YOU CHECK ITS BLOOD PRESSURE?

PROFESSOR! LOOK!

ITS BLOOD PRESSURE IS INDICATING THAT IT HASN'T LOST ANY BLOOD!

IT EVEN LOOKS LIKE IT'S GOT TOO MUCH! LOOK HOW SWOLLEN ITS VEINS ARE!

SO, WHAT CAN I DO?

YOU CAN GO TO BED. WE DON'T NEED YOU . . .

?

The next morning...

I KNOW YOU DIDN'T GET MUCH SLEEP LAST NIGHT, BUT THAT'S NO REASON TO PUT OFF TODAY'S TEST.

ESPECIALLY SINCE THE TEST IS PRETTY EASY! ALL YOU HAVE TO DO IS IDENTIFY THE TYPE OF LEPUS CORNUTUS YOU HAVE IN FRONT OF YOU.

MINE'S A WOLPERTINGER!

IT DOESN'T HAVE WINGS!

UH . . . I MEANT A JACKALOPE.

HMM!

SURE, I . . .

THANKS!

!

LOOK, SORCELINE— A VAMPIROVITCH! DO YOU KNOW WHAT THAT IS?

YES, IT'S THE CHILD OF A VAMPIRE AND A HUMAN. THEY HAVE A SIXTH SENSE THAT ALLOWS THEM TO DETECT VAMPIRES ANYWHERE IN THE WORLD.

73

THAT'S WHY YOU KNEW RIGHT AWAY THAT MADAME S. WAS A VAMPIRE.

MERODE! INSTEAD OF CHATTING, I'D RATHER YOU TELL US WHAT TYPE OF CREATURE YOU'RE HOLDING.

WINGS, ANTLERS, FANGS, AND A COCKSCOMB . . .

IT'S A WOLPERTINGER, PROFESSOR.

AND MINE'S A SKVADER!

WELL DONE, WILLA.

I CAN'T BE A VAMPIROVITCH. THEY DON'T HAVE THE POWER TO TURN PEOPLE INTO GLASS!

YOU'RE RIGHT.

SORCELINE! IT'S YOUR TURN! I'M LISTENING!

MY CREATURE IS . . .

. . . I . . .

?

74

AREN'T YOU GOING TO GO AFTER HER?

PFF! WHY, SHOULD I? SHE KEEPS LITTLE SECRETS.

BUT, GO AHEAD...

...I'M SURE SHE'LL—

?

SORCELINE? YOU OK?

I JUST... I WAS HOLDING THE HARE... BUT I DIDN'T FEEL ANY MAGIC IN IT!

I'VE LOST MY GIFT... AND WILLA DOESN'T WANT TO TALK TO ME ANYMORE!

THAT'S NOT SURPRISING. SHE CAN BE DIFFICULT!

YOU KNOW, THERE'S NO ONE HERE WHO CARES ABOUT YOU AS MUCH AS I DO...

DO YOU SEE WILLA RUNNING OUT HERE TO SEE HOW YOU ARE? OR MERODE? DO YOU THINK HE CARES ABOUT HOW YOU'RE FEELING?

YOU CAN COUNT ON ME, SORCELINE.

IT'S TRUE WHAT WILLA SAID. I'M YOUR KNIGHT IN SHINING ARMOR.

DON'T LOOK AT ME LIKE THAT. I'M NOT CRAZY! OTHER THAN CRAZY FOR YOU, AS THEY SAY IN THE MOVIES!

I CAN'T HELP IT, IT'S THE WAY YOU LOOK AT ME.

THE WAY I LOOK AT YOU IS NOTHING SPECIAL, ALCIDE. YOU'RE READING TOO MUCH INTO IT . . .

LOOKS LIKE WE'RE FEELING BETTER, HM?

COME ON, LOVEBIRDS, WE'RE GOING ON AN EXCURSION.

TO WHERE?

DID YOU HEAR THAT, SORCELINE? HE CALLED US LOVEBIRDS . . .

THAT'S RIGHT, WILLA. WE'RE GOING TO TRY AND FIND THE MOTHER OF THE DRAGON YOU'RE HEALING.

OH, RATS!

I FORGOT THE LIQUID BIOFUGE.

I'LL GO GET IT FOR YOU, PROFESSOR!

AND TELL ALCIDE TO HURRY UP!

PROFESSOR, I'M REALLY SORRY ABOUT RUNNING OUT ON THE TEST . . .

THE TEST YOU PASSED PERFECTLY!

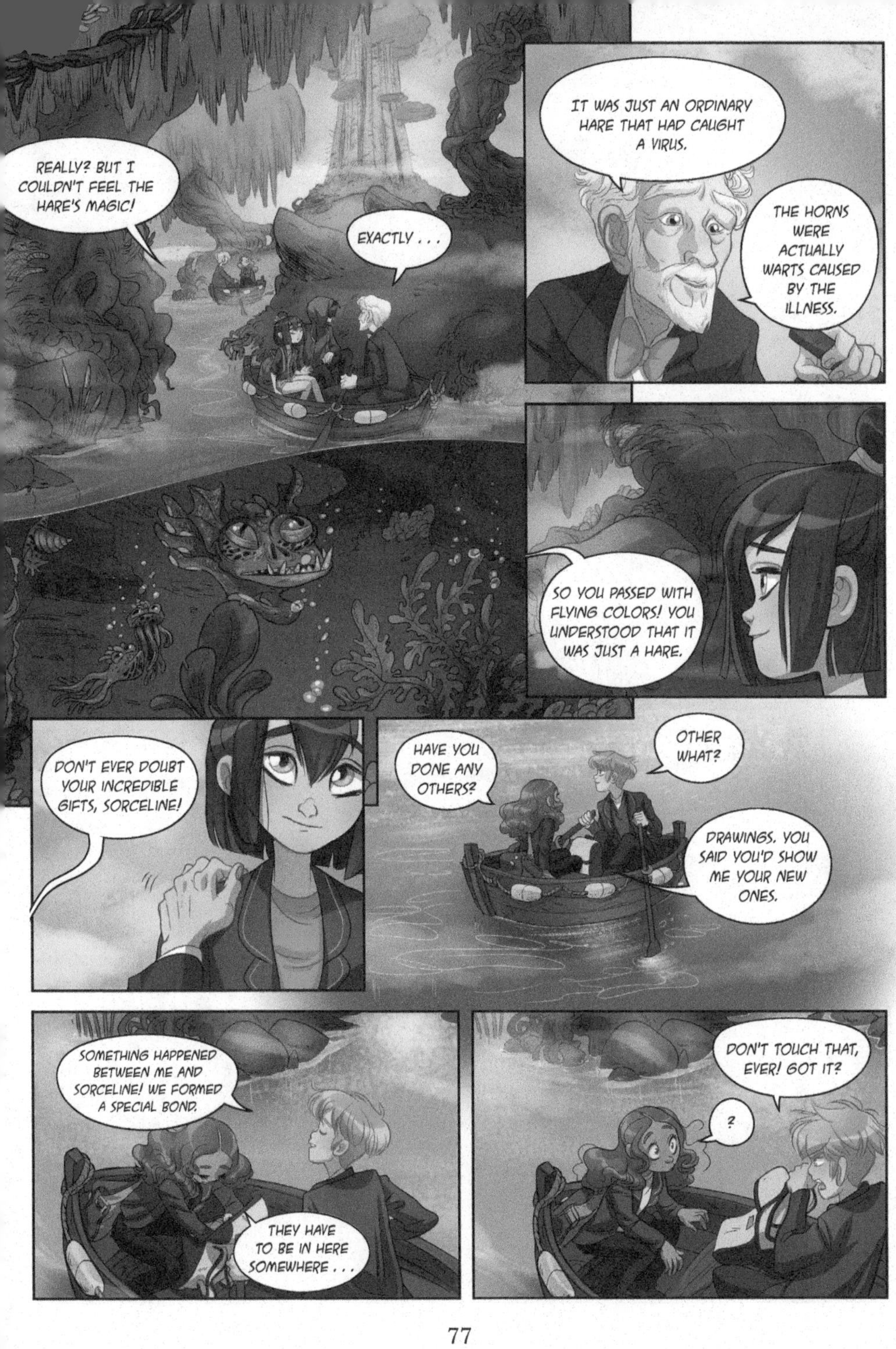

REALLY? BUT I COULDN'T FEEL THE HARE'S MAGIC!
EXACTLY . . .
IT WAS JUST AN ORDINARY HARE THAT HAD CAUGHT A VIRUS.
THE HORNS WERE ACTUALLY WARTS CAUSED BY THE ILLNESS.
SO YOU PASSED WITH FLYING COLORS! YOU UNDERSTOOD THAT IT WAS JUST A HARE.
DON'T EVER DOUBT YOUR INCREDIBLE GIFTS, SORCELINE!
HAVE YOU DONE ANY OTHERS?
OTHER WHAT?
DRAWINGS. YOU SAID YOU'D SHOW ME YOUR NEW ONES.
SOMETHING HAPPENED BETWEEN ME AND SORCELINE! WE FORMED A SPECIAL BOND.
THEY HAVE TO BE IN HERE SOMEWHERE . . .
DON'T TOUCH THAT, EVER! GOT IT?
?

LOOK! THE BLACKENED ENTRANCE TO THE CAVE PROVES THAT IT'S A DRAGON'S DEN.

I CAN'T WAIT TO SEE IT.

DON'T COUNT ON IT! YOU'RE ALL TOO INEXPERIENCED TO FACE AN ADULT DRAGON. EVEN IF IT'S ASLEEP!

IN THE MEANTIME, LOOK FOR ANY SIGNS OF LIFE IN THE BONES AND DEBRIS HERE ON THE GROUND.

SOME OF THEM MAY NOT BE REMAINS BUT THE BONES OF LIVING CREATURES SICK WITH RONGEOLE—A CONDITION THAT EATS THE SKIN AWAY!

YOU ALL KNOW HOW TO USE THIS LIQUID . . .

MERODE, PLEASE GIVE EVERYONE A VIAL OF LIQUID BIOFUGE.

. . . YOU SAW IT IN THE CLASSROOM. IF IT FOAMS, IT MEANS THERE IS LIFE!

?

HEY, LET ME GO! WHAT DO YOU WANT?

DID YOU CURSE THE HORNED HARE DURING THE TEST?

WHAT? NO! WHY?

BECAUSE . . . LOOK!

I FOUND IT WHEN I WENT BACK INTO THE ROOM. IT HAD TURNED TO GLASS.

HUH? BUT . . .

?

THAT'S AWFUL!!!

BUT . . . I DIDN'T SAY ANYTHING. NOT A WORD . . . I JUST THOUGHT IT.

I'M SORRY. I DIDN'T MEAN TO MAKE YOU CRY.

I'M A MONSTER!

NO, THAT'S NOT TRUE! DON'T SAY THAT!

THIS CAN'T GO ON. I HAVE TO ADMIT EVERYTHING.

I'D RATHER THAT THAN END UP TURNING ALL MY FRIENDS TO GLASS . . .

DON'T DO THAT! YOU'LL BE EXPELLED . . .

THAT WON'T HAPPEN IF YOU LEARN HOW TO CONTROL YOUR POWER . . .

BE PATIENT! YOU CAN DO IT! I'M HERE AND CAN HELP YOU!

I've run out of patience. I don't want it to keep happening . . .

NOOOOOOOO!

Besides, people will start to notice I'm feeling guilty.

MY GOODNESS, WHO WOULD DO THAT?

I think Willa's starting to figure out it's me . . .

REALLY? SHE WAS CRYING EARLIER, BUT WHY?

NO IDEA! IT MUST HAVE BEEN MERODE WHO MADE HER CRY!

She knows! I'm sure of it!

WHAT'S THEIR SECRET? I NEED TO KNOW!

I GUESS YOU'LL HAVE TO STOP AVOIDING HER, THEN . . .

It's like she's trying to get me to admit it . . .

I'LL TALK TO HER AGAIN IF SHE APOLOGIZES FOR HAVING SHARED A SECRET WITH MERODE INSTEAD OF ME!

Give her what she wants! Give her a hint!

I GUESS SHE'S NOT READY TO MAKE AMENDS.

PEOPLE RUN AWAY WHEN THEY FEEL GUILTY! SHE'S SHOWING ME SHE FEELS GUILTY.

I knew it!

. . . IT'S ALL MY FAULT!

I knew she would get it . . .

I KNOW.

AS THE SAYING GOES, A MISTAKE SHARED IS A MISTAKE HALVED.

SORT OF . . . BUT . . . THIS IS A BIG MISTAKE!

NOW, NOW! NO ONE'S DIED OR ANYTHING! YOU HID THINGS FROM ME AND SHARED THEM WITH MERODE . . .

BUT YOU'VE APOLOGIZED. THAT'S THE MOST IMPORTANT THING. I FORGIVE YOU.

UH . . . ARE WE TALKING ABOUT THE SAME THING?

OF COURSE. WHAT ELSE COULD WE BE TALKING ABOUT?

?

ARE YOU MAD?

YOU'RE RIGHT TO STAY AWAY FROM ME! I'M A MONSTER!

THAT'S THE SILLIEST THING I'VE EVER HEARD!

?

HOW DID MERODE KNOW YOU WERE THE ONE PETRIFYING PEOPLE?

I . . . I DON'T KNOW! I HAVEN'T THOUGHT ABOUT IT.

HOW COULD ANYONE TELL IT WAS YOU? YOU WERE NEVER ALONE WHEN YOU CURSED THEM.

WE NEED TO ACTUALLY PROVE THAT IT'S YOU WHO IS PETRIFYING PEOPLE.

TO DO THAT, YOU HAVE TO CURSE SOMEONE WHEN YOU'RE ALONE!

OK! BUT WHO?

THE ONLY PERSON I DON'T SUSPECT . . .

PROFESSOR BALZAR!

HUH?

ARE YOU NUTS? I COULD NEVER DO THAT!

YOU HAVE TO! FIND A WAY TO START AN ARGUMENT!

WHAT? YOU WANT TO DROP OUT AND GO HOME?!

"COUGH COUGH COUGH COUGH"

CALM DOWN, PROFESSOR!

GRRR! CALM DOWN?! AFTER WHAT YOU JUST SAID?!

YOU SEEMED SO PASSIONATE! YOU DON'T WANT TO BE A CRYPTOZOOLOGIST ANYMORE? WHAT HAPPENED?

ARE YOU REALLY READY TO WALK AWAY FROM THIS PUZZLE?

?

WHAT IS IT?

THE YOUNG DRAGON'S BLOOD.

BUT THAT'S IMPOSSIBLE! DRAGON'S BLOOD IS—

RED! JUST LIKE ITS MOTHER'S, WHICH I DREW THIS AFTERNOON.

THE STRANGE COLOR MUST HAVE SOMETHING TO DO WITH THE ATTACK OF THE LULLABIS . . .

MAYBE THE LULLABIS HAD AN ILLNESS THAT THEY TRANSFERRED TO THE DRAGON WHEN THEY BIT IT.

LIKE MOSQUITOS AND HUMANS.

YES. SO, WE NEED TO CATCH SOME OF THESE LULLABIS AND TEST THEM.

PROFESSOR, WAS THE DRAGON IN CONTACT WITH A CALADRIUS?

NO.

THEN WE HAVE TO HURRY UP AND CATCH ONE!

HEH HEH!

WE'RE NOT IN KINDERGARTEN HERE! STOP PLAYING AROUND AND FIND A WAY TO GET ANGRY, WILL YOU?

OH, BACK SO SOON?

85

PROFESSOR?

HMMM?

WHO AM I?

?

NOW'S NOT THE TIME FOR THAT. COME HERE AND TAKE A LOOK AT WHAT I FOUND OUT ABOUT THE LULLABIS . . .

WHO AM I?

I DON'T KNOW. YOU NEED TO FIND OUT FOR YOURSELF!

BUT YOU KNOW ABOUT ME SINCE YOU KNEW I WAS ADOPTED.

TRUE. BUT IT'S MORE COMPLICATED THAN THAT!

SO, TELL ME WHO I AM!

CURSE YOU! CURSE YOU TO THE END OF TIME!!!!

I CAN'T, SORCELINE . . .

TELL ME! TELL ME NOW OR I'LL . . .

DON'T WORRY! HE'LL UNDERSTAND LATER WHY YOU ACTED LIKE THAT!

Balzar hasn't spoken to me in two days. I'm sad about it, but relieved that he hasn't turn into glass!

Willa and I are super happy. This proves that I'm innocent . . .

THAT DOESN'T PROVE ANYTHING!

YES, IT DOES!

LOOK! IT'S AN ADELIT! IT'S RARE TO SEE ONE DURING THE DAY. IT MUST BE THIS TERRIBLE WEATHER THAT'S BROUGHT IT OUT . . .

I DON'T CARE ABOUT YOUR ADELIT! I'M NOT THE ONE TURNING PEOPLE TO GLASS! IT'S NOT ME!

THINK . . .

WHO WAS ALWAYS THERE, OTHER THAN ME, WHEN SORCELINE CURSED PEOPLE?

. . . MERODE AND ALCIDE!

OH! ALCIDE'S NOTEBOOK . . .

WHY DO YOU INSIST ON ACCUSING ME?

YOU WANT PROOF THAT I'M INNOCENT?

CURSE YOU!

THINK OF WHAT YOU'RE SAYING!

CURSE YOU, MERODE!

WELL SAID, SORCELINE! DO YOU WANT ME TO DEAL WITH HIM?

YOU'LL NEVER GUESS WHAT I FOUND IN ALCIDE'S THINGS.

THERE'S TONS OF THEM! THESE DON'T LOOK LIKE DRAWINGS BY A GUY WITH A CRUSH, SORCELINE . . .

IT'S MORE THAN THAT!

HE'S DOESN'T JUST LIKE YOU, HE'S OBSESSED!

HE COULD BE A SYLPH, DON'T YOU THINK?

ALCIDE? IMPOSSIBLE!

HE LOVED YOU THE SECOND HE LAID EYES ON YOU. HE DECLARED HIS DEVOTION TO YOU AND VOWED TO PROTECT YOU FOREVER!

BUT WHY DIDN'T I SENSE IT?

WELL, WE'LL SOON FIND OUT . . .

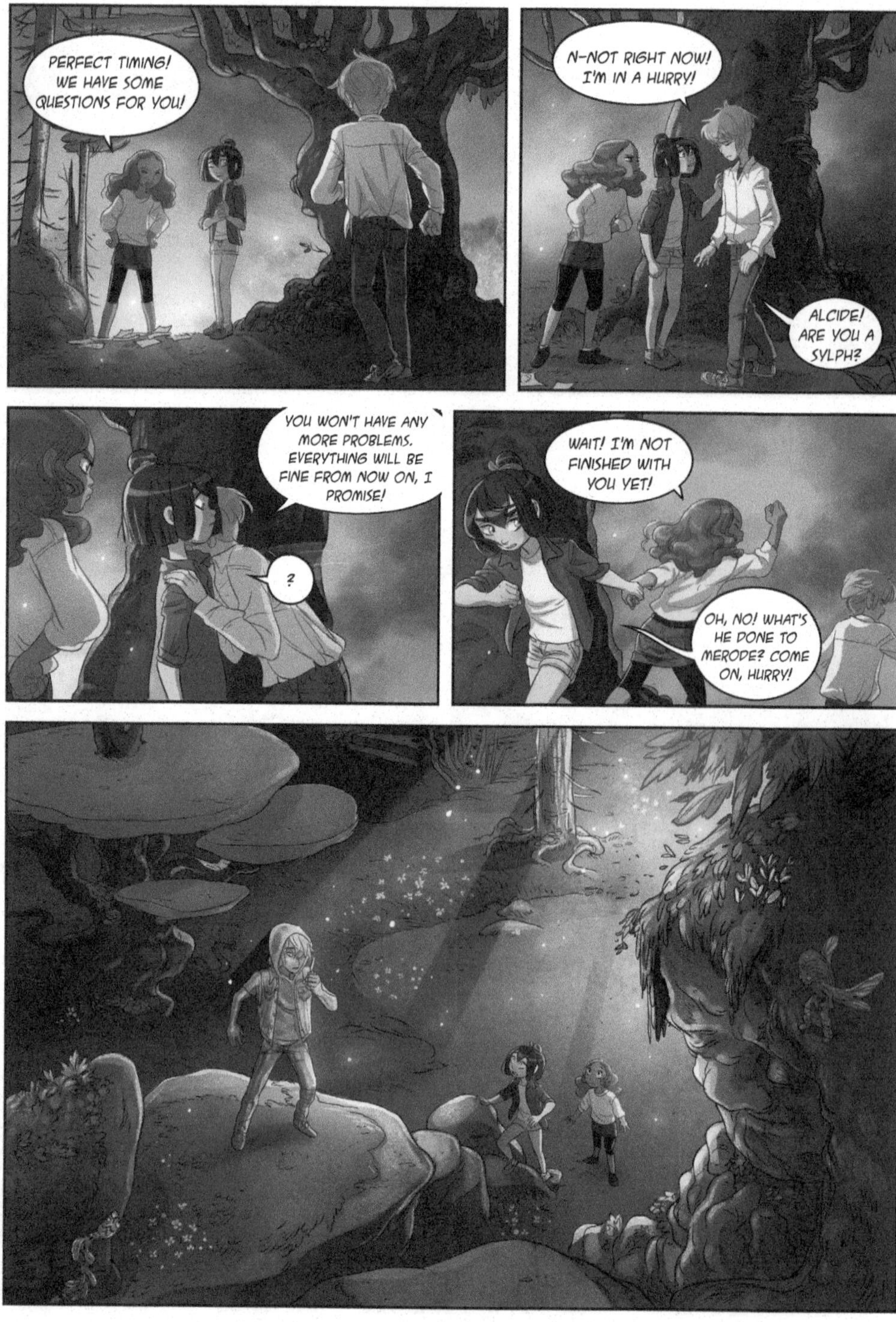
PERFECT TIMING! WE HAVE SOME QUESTIONS FOR YOU!
N-NOT RIGHT NOW! I'M IN A HURRY!
ALCIDE! ARE YOU A SYLPH?
YOU WON'T HAVE ANY MORE PROBLEMS. EVERYTHING WILL BE FINE FROM NOW ON, I PROMISE!
?
WAIT! I'M NOT FINISHED WITH YOU YET!
OH, NO! WHAT'S HE DONE TO MERODE? COME ON, HURRY!

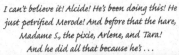

I can't believe it! Alcide! He's been doing this! He just petrified Merode! And before that the hare, Madame S., the pixie, Arlene, and Tara! And he did all that because he's . . .

A SYLPH WHO FELL FOR SORCELINE.

WE SHOULD HAVE FIGURED IT OUT! THE FIRST DAY, IN THE LOCKER ROOM, HE ALREADY SEEMED OBSESSED WITH ME . . .

WHEN HE FOCUSED HIS DEVOTION ON SORCELINE, HE SWORE TO PROTECT HER.

SO, WHENEVER I CURSED SOMEONE, HE THOUGHT I WANTED THEM TO LEAVE ME ALONE FOREVER, SO HE PETRIFIED THEM . . .

SO, ACTUALLY, THE GORGON HAS NOTHING TO DO WITH THE ATTACKS.

LET'S TRY AND FIND OUT HOW HE WAS ABLE TO DO IT WITHOUT SORCELINE SENSING HIS POWER . . .

?

Who could be banging on the trap door? There's no one down there except the statues! Unless . . .

91

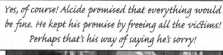

Yes, of course! Alcide promised that everything would be fine. He kept his promise by freeing all the victims! Perhaps that's his way of saying he's sorry!

HE MUST HAVE TURNED HIMSELF INTO A GLASS STATUE, THEREBY RELEASING YOU FROM THE SPELL.

SO, WE'RE BACK TO OUR NORMAL SELVES?

BUT WHY DIDN'T IT WORK FOR MERODE?

ALCIDE'S HATRED FOR HIM WAS TOO STRONG! STRONGER THAN THE REVERSAL MAGIC!

OH TARA, I'M SO HAPPY TO SEE YOU BACK IN THE FLESH!

OW! GENTLY! I FEEL LIKE I'VE BEEN SHATTERED . . . THEN GLUED BACK TOGETHER!

REALLY? ME TOO!

HEH HEH. CHALLENGES BRING PEOPLE TOGETHER!

I NEVER THOUGHT I'D SAY THIS, BUT I'M REALLY HAPPY TO SEE YOU TWO!

If we could only find out what kind of magic Alcide used to petrify his victims . . .

. . . WE COULD FREE MERODE! AND THEN WE WOULD ALL BE TOGETHER AGAIN, LIKE WHEN WE STARTED!

AAAAAAAAAHHH!

OOPS!

ARCHIBALD! MY KITCHEN!!!

Uh . . . as long as Professor Balzar stays out of Madame S.'s kitchen!

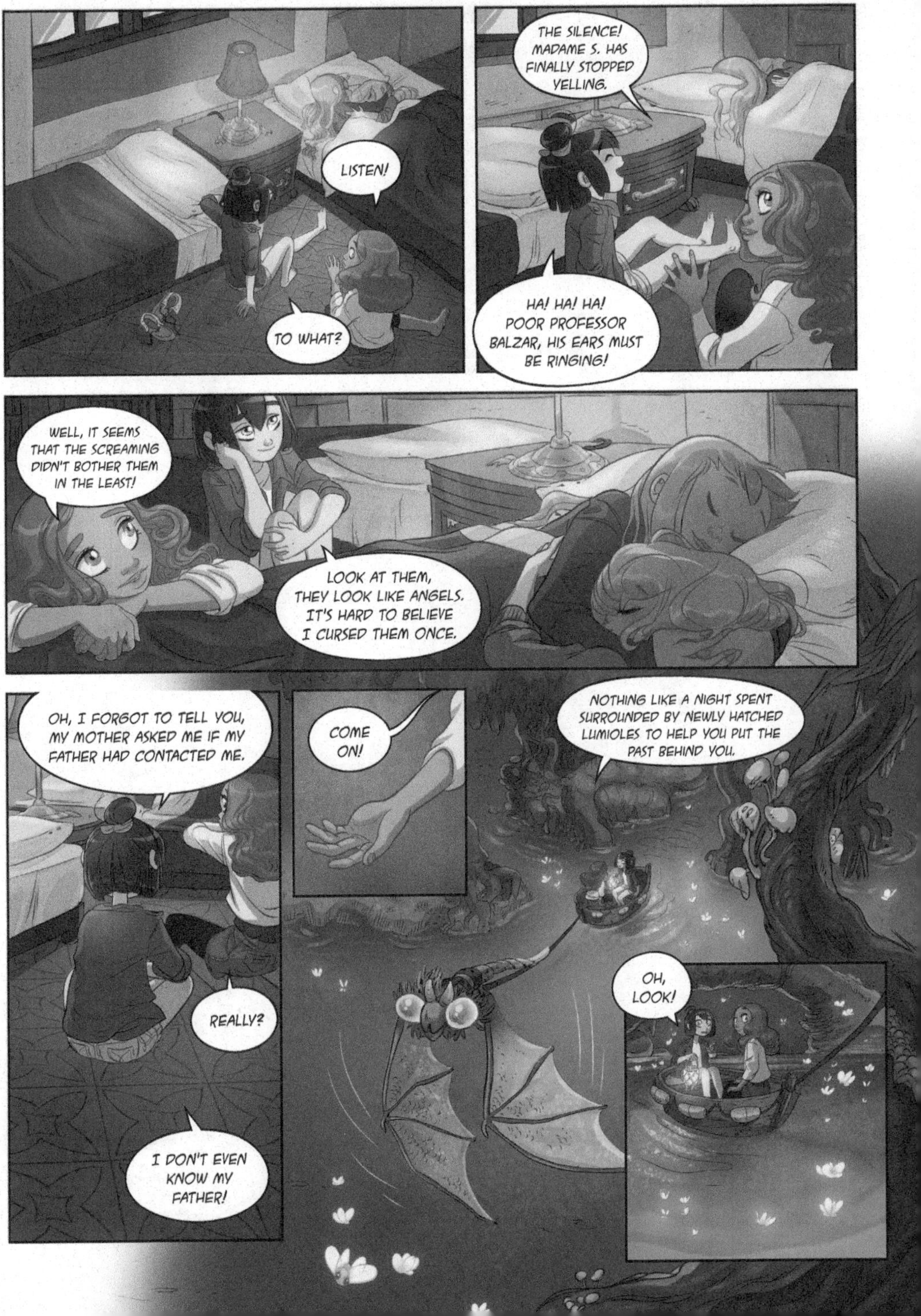
LISTEN!
TO WHAT?
THE SILENCE! MADAME S. HAS FINALLY STOPPED YELLING.
HA! HA! HA! POOR PROFESSOR BALZAR, HIS EARS MUST BE RINGING!
WELL, IT SEEMS THAT THE SCREAMING DIDN'T BOTHER THEM IN THE LEAST!
LOOK AT THEM, THEY LOOK LIKE ANGELS. IT'S HARD TO BELIEVE I CURSED THEM ONCE.
OH, I FORGOT TO TELL YOU, MY MOTHER ASKED ME IF MY FATHER HAD CONTACTED ME.
REALLY?
I DON'T EVEN KNOW MY FATHER!
COME ON!
NOTHING LIKE A NIGHT SPENT SURROUNDED BY NEWLY HATCHED LUMIOLES TO HELP YOU PUT THE PAST BEHIND YOU.
OH, LOOK!

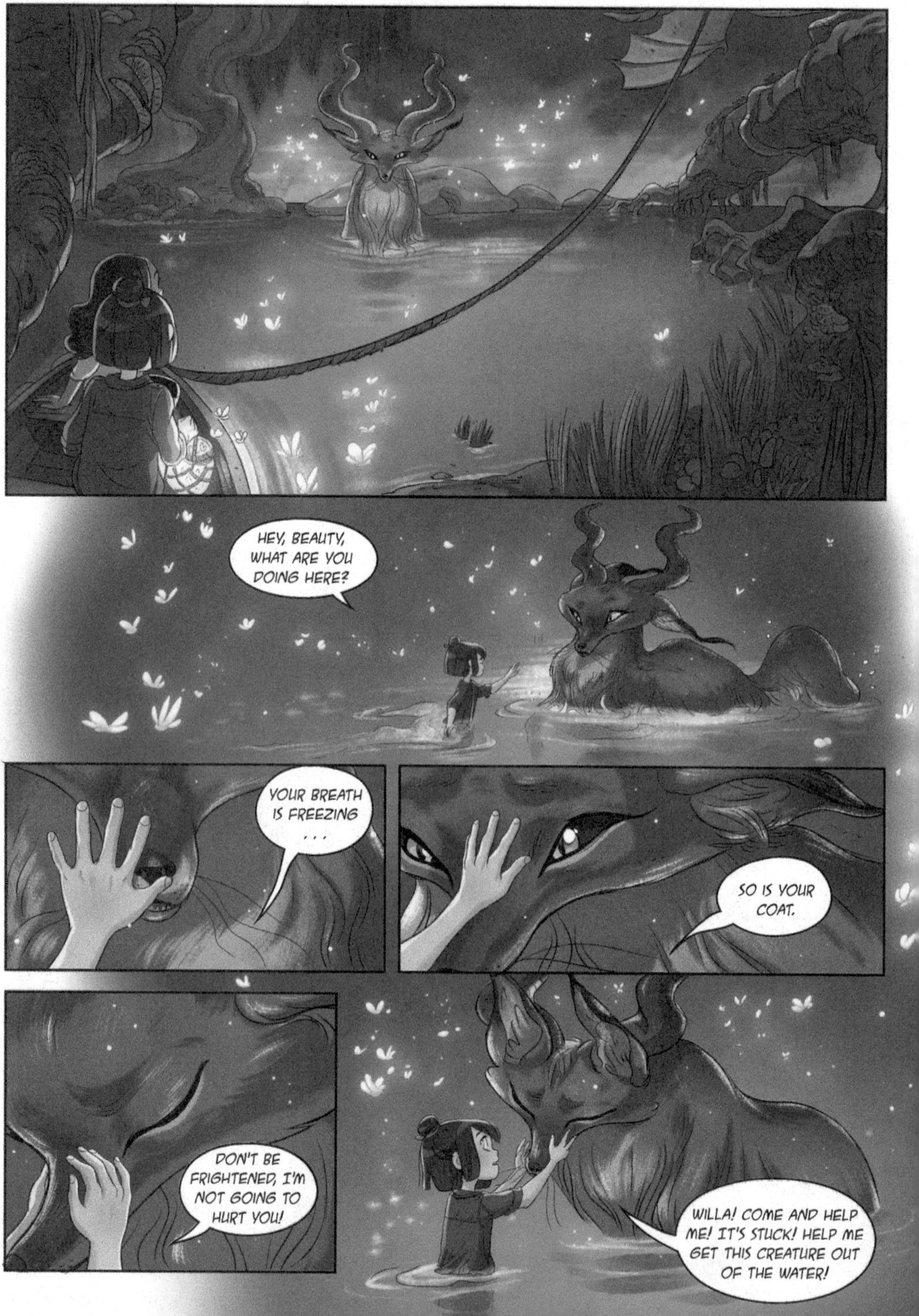
HEY, BEAUTY, WHAT ARE YOU DOING HERE?
YOUR BREATH IS FREEZING . . .
SO IS YOUR COAT.
DON'T BE FRIGHTENED, I'M NOT GOING TO HURT YOU!
WILLA! COME AND HELP ME! IT'S STUCK! HELP ME GET THIS CREATURE OUT OF THE WATER!

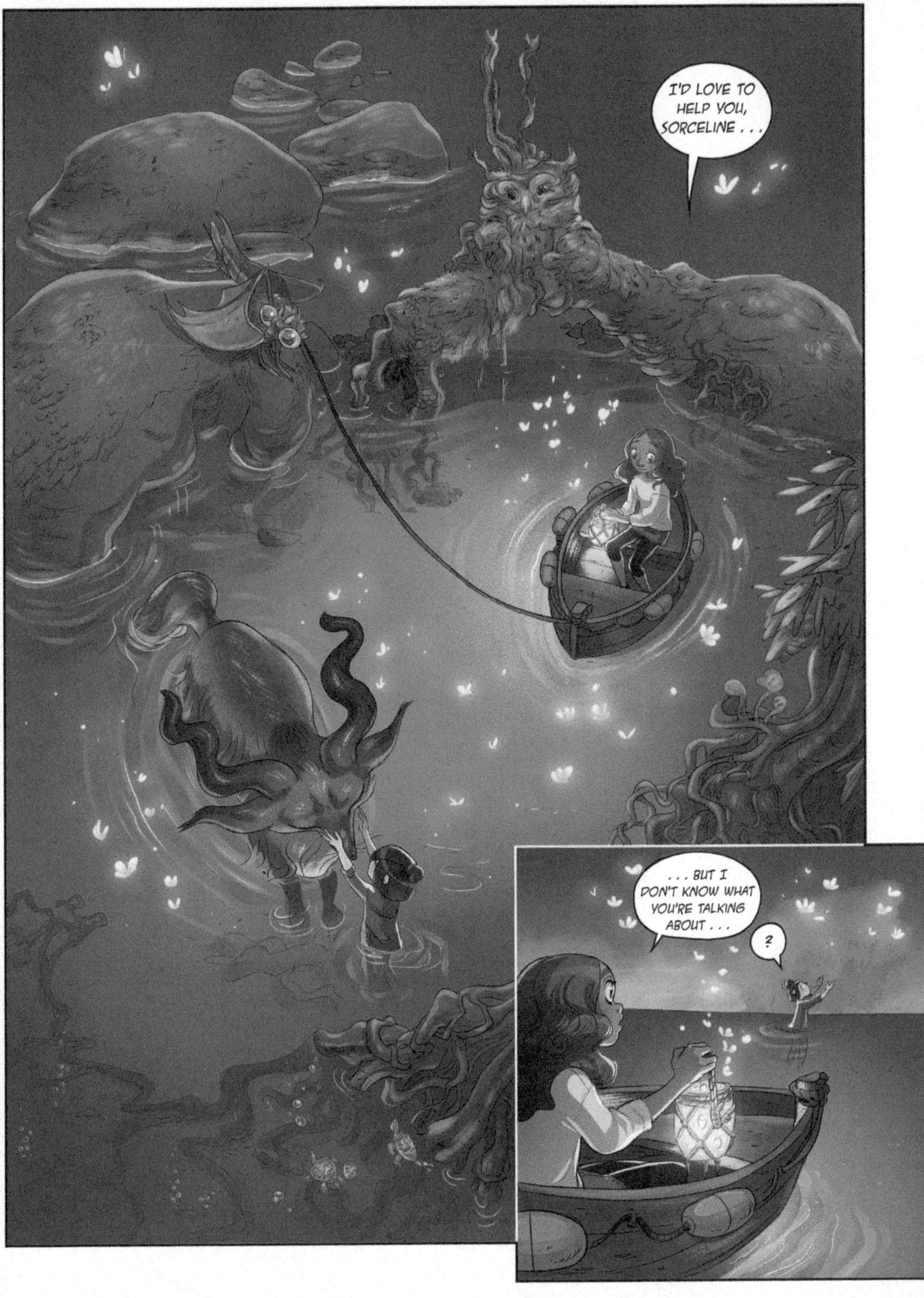
I'D LOVE TO HELP YOU, SORCELINE . . .
. . . BUT I DON'T KNOW WHAT YOU'RE TALKING ABOUT . . .
?

Part 3

For several days, I've been seeing a creature that no one else sees ...

I don't know why. Maybe it's a spirit that's stuck on the Isle of Vorn ... Or maybe it's a guardian angel sent to protect me from some imminent danger ...

Or a guide meant to show me who I really am ...

I could sit here all day, watching it, but I have work to do ...

We're planning a reenactment.

SO, YOU WANT ME TO BE ALCIDE, IS THAT RIGHT?

YES, PROFESSOR. ON THE NIGHT TARA WAS PETRIFIED, I WAS UP AHEAD, SORCELINE WAS BEHIND ME, AND ALCIDE WAS LAST.

I CAN GO LAST INSTEAD.

I'M GOING TO TRY AND SEE, YOU KNOW, THE CREATURE THAT ONLY I SEE!

YOU CAN'T! YOU HAVE TO STAY IN THE MIDDLE! A CRIME REENACTMENT NEEDS TO BE EXACTLY THAT—A PERFECT REENACTMENT. IT'S THE ONLY WAY WE'RE GOING TO FIND OUT HOW ALCIDE PETRIFIED TARA.

LOOK! EVEN THE PIXIES ARE ATTENDING THE REENACTMENT!

EXCELLENT. THIS SLEEPY LITTLE PIXIE HAS ARRIVED AT EXACTLY THE SAME TIME SHE DID THAT NIGHT!

AND SHE'S PLAYING THE ZOMBIE PERFECTLY, DREAMING WITH HER EYES OPEN!

ARLENE SHOULD BE SCREAMING ANY SECOND NOW!

NOT YET! ALCIDE SCREAMED FIRST . . .

OW!

EXACTLY, PROFESSOR! HOW DID YOU GUESS?

HMMPH! I DIDN'T DO IT ON PURPOSE! THE PIXIE MUST HAVE MISTOOK MY LEG FOR A CRUNCHY REED.

IF MY CALCULATIONS ARE RIGHT . . . THREE, TWO, ONE, AND . . .

AAAAAAAARGH!

RIGHT ON TIME!

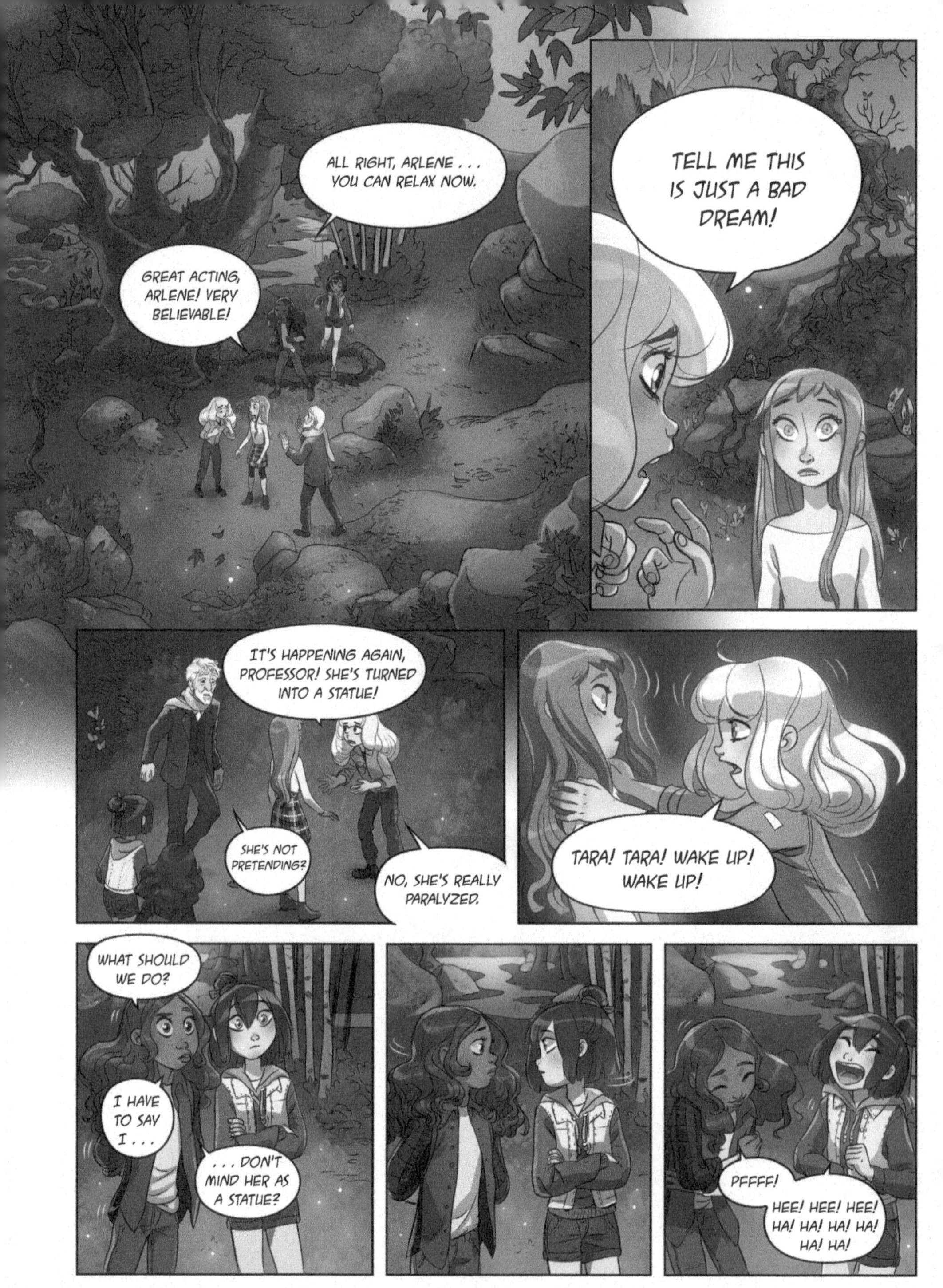
ALL RIGHT, ARLENE . . . YOU CAN RELAX NOW.
GREAT ACTING, ARLENE! VERY BELIEVABLE!
TELL ME THIS IS JUST A BAD DREAM!
IT'S HAPPENING AGAIN, PROFESSOR! SHE'S TURNED INTO A STATUE!
SHE'S NOT PRETENDING?
NO, SHE'S REALLY PARALYZED.
TARA! TARA! WAKE UP! WAKE UP!
WHAT SHOULD WE DO?
I HAVE TO SAY I . . .
. . . DON'T MIND HER AS A STATUE?
PFFFF!
HEE! HEE! HEE! HA! HA! HA! HA! HA! HA!

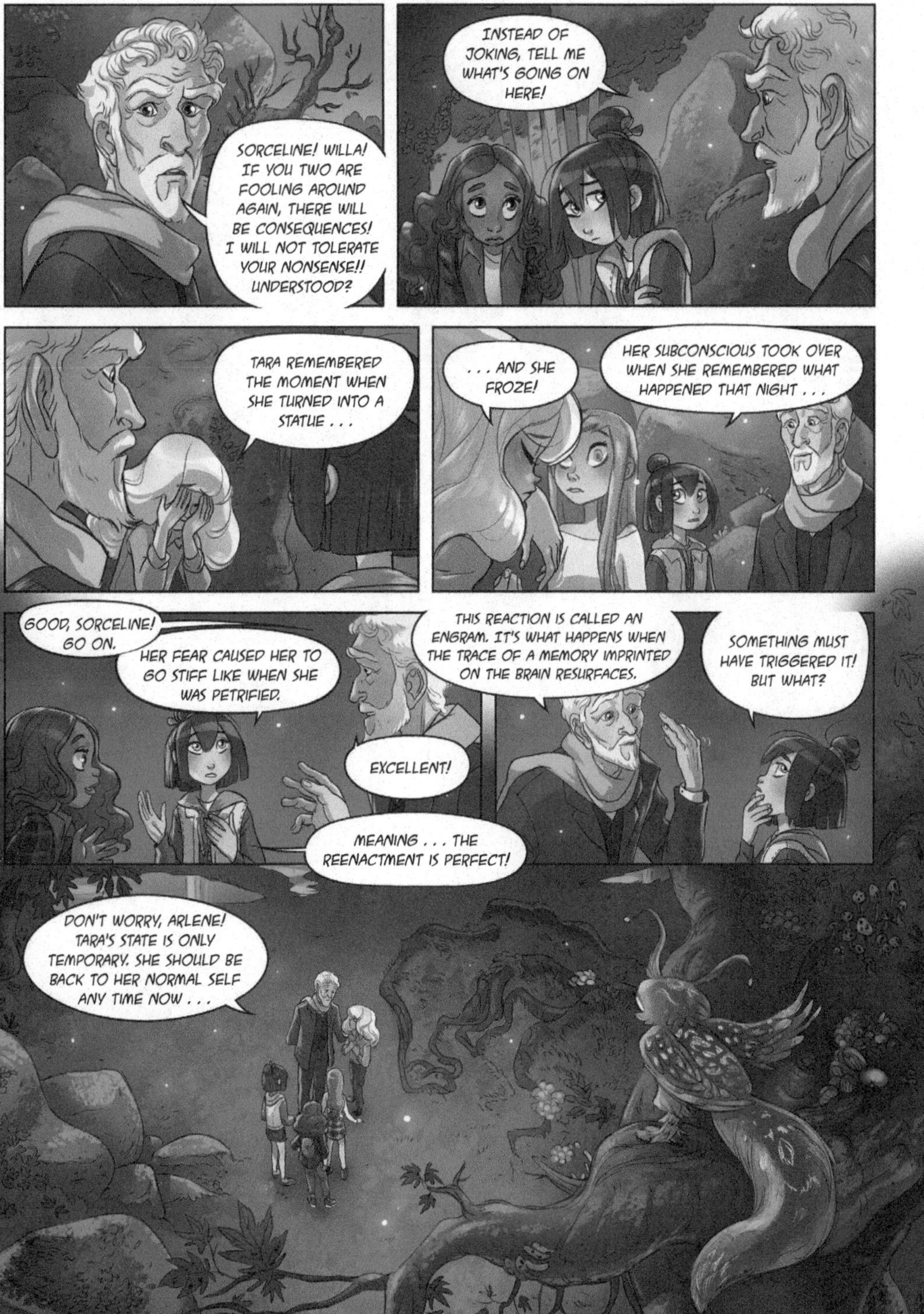
SORCELINE! WILLA! IF YOU TWO ARE FOOLING AROUND AGAIN, THERE WILL BE CONSEQUENCES! I WILL NOT TOLERATE YOUR NONSENSE!! UNDERSTOOD?
INSTEAD OF JOKING, TELL ME WHAT'S GOING ON HERE!
TARA REMEMBERED THE MOMENT WHEN SHE TURNED INTO A STATUE . . .
. . . AND SHE FROZE!
HER SUBCONSCIOUS TOOK OVER WHEN SHE REMEMBERED WHAT HAPPENED THAT NIGHT . . .
HER FEAR CAUSED HER TO GO STIFF LIKE WHEN SHE WAS PETRIFIED.
GOOD, SORCELINE! GO ON.
EXCELLENT!
MEANING . . . THE REENACTMENT IS PERFECT!
THIS REACTION IS CALLED AN ENGRAM. IT'S WHAT HAPPENS WHEN THE TRACE OF A MEMORY IMPRINTED ON THE BRAIN RESURFACES.
SOMETHING MUST HAVE TRIGGERED IT! BUT WHAT?
DON'T WORRY, ARLENE! TARA'S STATE IS ONLY TEMPORARY. SHE SHOULD BE BACK TO HER NORMAL SELF ANY TIME NOW . . .

Early the next morning...

BEFORE I FROZE, I THOUGHT I SAW MERODE STARING AT ME AND IT GAVE ME THE CREEPS!

YOU KNOW WHAT, TARA? I THINK MERODE'S SPIRIT MUST'VE CONNECTED TO—

TO MINE!

YES, THAT'S IT! MERODE TOOK ADVANTAGE OF YOUR STATE—

TO COMMUNICATE WITH ME!

EXACTLY! HE PROBABLY HAS INFORMATION FOR—

FOR US! HE MAY BE ABLE TO TELL US HOW TO FREE HIM.

OR HE KNOWS WHERE—

ALCIDE'S STATUE IS!

DO YOU REALIZE THAT—

I FINISH YOUR SENTENCES?

YES, WELL DONE!

PROFESSOR BALZAR!

YES?

MAY I SPEAK WITH YOU ALONE?

SORCELINE . . .

YOU'RE NOT GOING TO TELL HIM ABOUT THE HALLUCINATIONS, ARE YOU?

THE WHAT?

ARCHIBALD! CHILDREN! HURRY AND COME WITH ME!

103

LOOK! IT'S A SKELETON! IT MUST HAVE CRAWLED TOWARDS THE MANOR! I THINK IT HAS RONGEOLE.

WHO CAN TELL ME WHAT RONGEOLE IS?

IT'S . . .

IT'S A CONDITION THAT CAUSES SKIN TO DECAY.

BRAVO TARA! YOU'VE EARNED THE RIGHT TO HEAL THIS BEING.

I'M PARTICULARLY PROUD OF YOU BECAUSE YOU WEREN'T AROUND WHEN I TALKED ABOUT THIS ILLNESS IN CLASS.

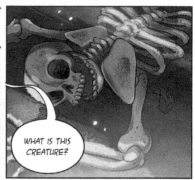

WHAT IS THIS CREATURE?

IT'S CLEARLY A HUMAN . . .

BUT IT'S STRANGE!

WHAT IS?

HOW DID A HUMAN GET ON THE ISLAND WITHOUT THE BOOK?

WHAT BOOK?

OH, NEVER MIND ... WE'LL USE THE ENCHANTED SERPENT'S HEALING ABILITIES.

THIS PERSON MUST HAVE ARRIVED HERE LIKE WE DID ...

WEIRD! I CAN'T EVEN REMEMBER HOW I GOT ON THE ISLAND ...

HA! HA! VERY FUNNY!

NO, REALLY! TELL ME! WHERE WERE YOU BEFORE YOU GOT ON THE BOAT, SMARTY?

OH ... YOU'RE RIGHT! I'M DRAWING A BLANK.

YOU SEE? ASK PROFESSOR BALZAR!

NO! WAIT! I'LL CHECK MY PHONE, IT WOULD'VE TRACKED MY LOCATION.

I DON'T HAVE A SIGNAL!

OF COURSE NOT! DIDN'T YOU READ THE RULES? WE'RE CUT OFF FROM THE REST OF THE WORLD!

BUT ... HOW DID SORCELINE CALL HER MOTHER AND RECEIVE A MESSAGE FROM HER?

LOOK, SORCELINE! SINCE WE'VE BEEN HERE, YOU HAVE NOT RECEIVED ANY CALLS OR MESSAGES ON YOUR PHONE!

HUH?

HEY! HOW LONG DO I HAVE TO WAIT BEFORE YOU BRING ME THE SERPENT?

YOU CAN'T COUNT ON THEM, PROFESSOR. I'LL GET IT FOR YOU!

GIVE IT TO ME!

HURRY UP!

IN THE MEANTIME, I'LL EXPLAIN TO YOU HOW THIS SERPENT PROVIDES A CURE FOR RONGEOLE!

THE ENCHANTED SERPENT CAN STRETCH INDEFINITELY, AND IT CAN REPAIR ANYTHING IT TOUCHES.

THAT'S WHY WE'RE GOING TO WRAP THE SERPENT AROUND THE WHOLE SKELETON.

SO IT CAN REGENERATE THE SKELETON'S SKIN AND ORGANS.

PSHH! THAT DIDN'T EVEN HURT. I'M GETTING USED TO BEING ATTACKED!

POOR THING!

DON'T WORRY, THIS DOESN'T HURT THE SERPENT AT ALL. AND WHY IS THAT?

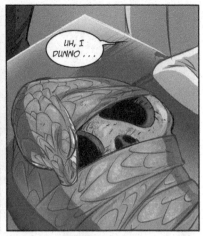

UH, I DUNNO . . .

. . . BECAUSE IT'S A PARASITE.

BECAUSE IT'S A PARASITE, PROFESSOR!

NO, TARA, THAT'S INCORRECT. IT'S SIMPLY BECAUSE IT FEEDS ON WOUNDS. IT LIKES WOUNDED BEINGS. THEY ALLOW IT TO SURVIVE.

BUT BRAVO ANYWAY!

GRRR . . .

MAKING MISTAKES IS ESSENTIAL FOR LEARNING!

PROFESSOR, MAY I SPEAK WITH YOU? IT'S URGENT!

YOU'LL PROBABLY FIND SOMETHING IN HERE ABOUT THE CREATURE YOU'RE SEEING.

The Great Book of Dream Interpretation

DECODE THE MESSAGES OF YOUR SUBCONSCIOUS!

OK, SO YOU AGREE WITH WILLA—THAT I'm HALLUCINATING!

OH, DEAR, WE'RE GROUCHY TODAY. DO I DETECT A HINT OF JEALOUSY?

WHAT'S THE POINT OF TELLING ME I HAVE SPECIAL POWERS . . .

. . . IF YOU'RE JUST GOING TO ACCUSE ME OF DAYDREAMING?

DREAMS AND HALLUCINATIONS ARE NOT THE SAME, SORCELINE . . .

SURE!

Dandyhog

?

The dandyhog represents happy memories buried deep in the past.

PROFESSOR, ARE YOU SURE THIS BOOK ONLY INCLUDES DREAM CREATURES?

ABSOLUTELY! NONE THAT EXIST IN REAL LIFE.

The Omen

DID YOU FIND SOMETHING?

UH . . .

The Omen

The Omen

WELL?

NO, NO, IT'S NOTHING!

ALCIDE WASN'T A HUMAN. HE WAS A SYLPH. THEY GET THEIR POWER FROM RUSHES OF EMOTION.

During our first excursion, Alcide was able to petrify Tara after a bout of pain . . .

. . . and he petrified Arlene after he spent the day with Sorceline.

On our second excursion, the shock of Professor Balzar's surprise must have given Alcide the energy he needed to petrify the pixie.

I'M NOT SURE WHAT EMOTIONS COULD'VE CAUSED HIM TO PETRIFY MADAME S. OR THE HORNED HARE . . .

BUT, IN YOUR CASE, MERODE, IT WAS OBVIOUSLY ANGER.

YOU AND SORCELINE ARGUED. SHE CURSED YOU AND YOU LEFT. ALCIDE FOLLOWED YOU. AND SINCE HE WAS ATTACKING EVERYONE . . .

. . . WHO SORCELINE WAS CURSING . . .

HE PETRIFIED YOU. YOU TRIED TO DEFEND YOURSELF WITH THE KNIFE.

THERE'S SOMETHING DIFFERENT ABOUT YOU, BUT I CAN'T FIGURE OUT WHAT IT IS . . .

SORCELINE, I DON'T HAVE TIME TO MESS AROUND!

OH, BECAUSE YOU'RE WORKING RIGHT NOW? AREN'T YOU SUPPOSED TO BE TRYING TO CATCH LULLABIS FOR YOUR DRAGON?

YEAH, BUT WHILE I WAS LOOKING, I CAME ACROSS MERODE.

DO YOU HAVE ANY IDEA HOW TO FREE HIM?

YES! REMEMBER HOW, JUST BEFORE TARA WAS STUNNED THIS MORNING...

. . . SHE FELT AN ICY CHILL?

IT'S LIKE SHE WAS LITERALLY FROZEN IN PLACE . . .

SO, THE PETRIFICATION PROCESS MUST BE SIMILAR TO HOW WATER TURNS TO ICE.

WHY IS MERODE THE ONLY ONE OF ALCIDE'S VICTIMS WHO'S STILL A STATUE?

TO REVERSE IT, THE STATUE NEEDS TO BE SUBJECTED TO HIGH HEAT!

HEY, YOU LISTENING?

YOU SAID IT WAS BECAUSE ALCIDE'S HATRED FOR MERODE WAS STRONGER THAN THE REVERSAL MAGIC. BUT I DON'T BELIEVE THAT ANYMORE.

LOOK! LULLABIS!

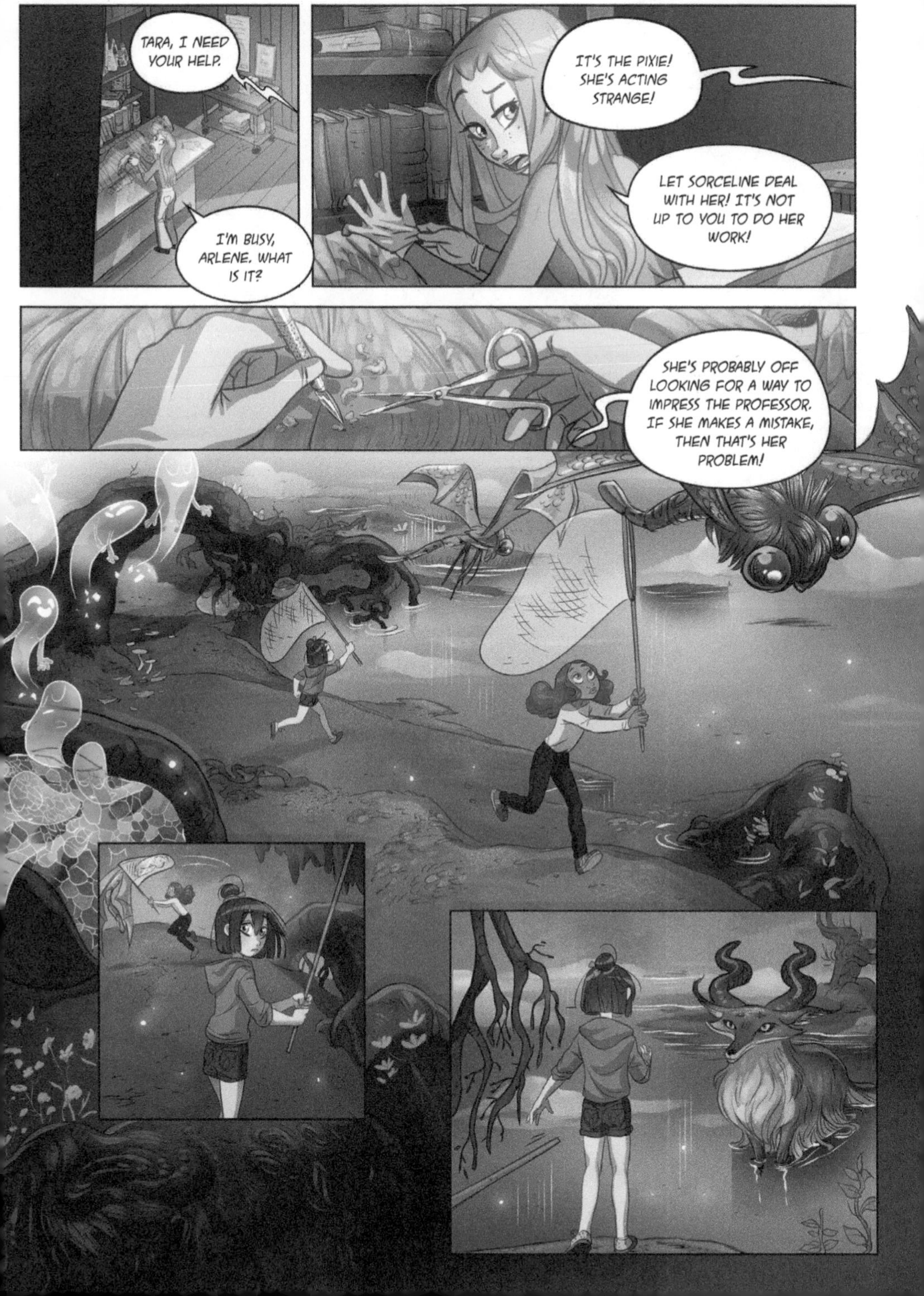
TARA, I NEED YOUR HELP.
I'M BUSY, ARLENE. WHAT IS IT?
IT'S THE PIXIE! SHE'S ACTING STRANGE!
LET SORCELINE DEAL WITH HER! IT'S NOT UP TO YOU TO DO HER WORK!
SHE'S PROBABLY OFF LOOKING FOR A WAY TO IMPRESS THE PROFESSOR. IF SHE MAKES A MISTAKE, THEN THAT'S HER PROBLEM!

TARA, DON'T TELL ME YOU'RE LETTING YOUR PERSONAL ISSUES GET IN THE WAY OF YOUR DUTY TO THE CREATURES...

GRRR... WHY IS SHE ALWAYS RIGHT?!

SHE'S FINE, SHE'S JUST SLEEPY!

...BUT LET'S LET SORCELINE TAKE CARE OF HER! AND TOO BAD IF SHE GETS IT WRONG!

WE CAN HELP EACH OTHER, DON'T YOU THINK?

I HAVE TO GET THAT ASSISTANT POSITION! YOU KNOW I'M MUCH BETTER OFF HERE THAN AT HOME...

YES, I KNOW. ...DO YOU WANT TO TALK ABOUT IT?

NO! AND BESIDES, EVER SINCE WE WERE FREED FROM THE SPELL, I'VE FELT LIKE SOMETHING HAS CHANGED IN ME...

...LIKE SOMEONE PUMPED ME FULL OF HOPE!

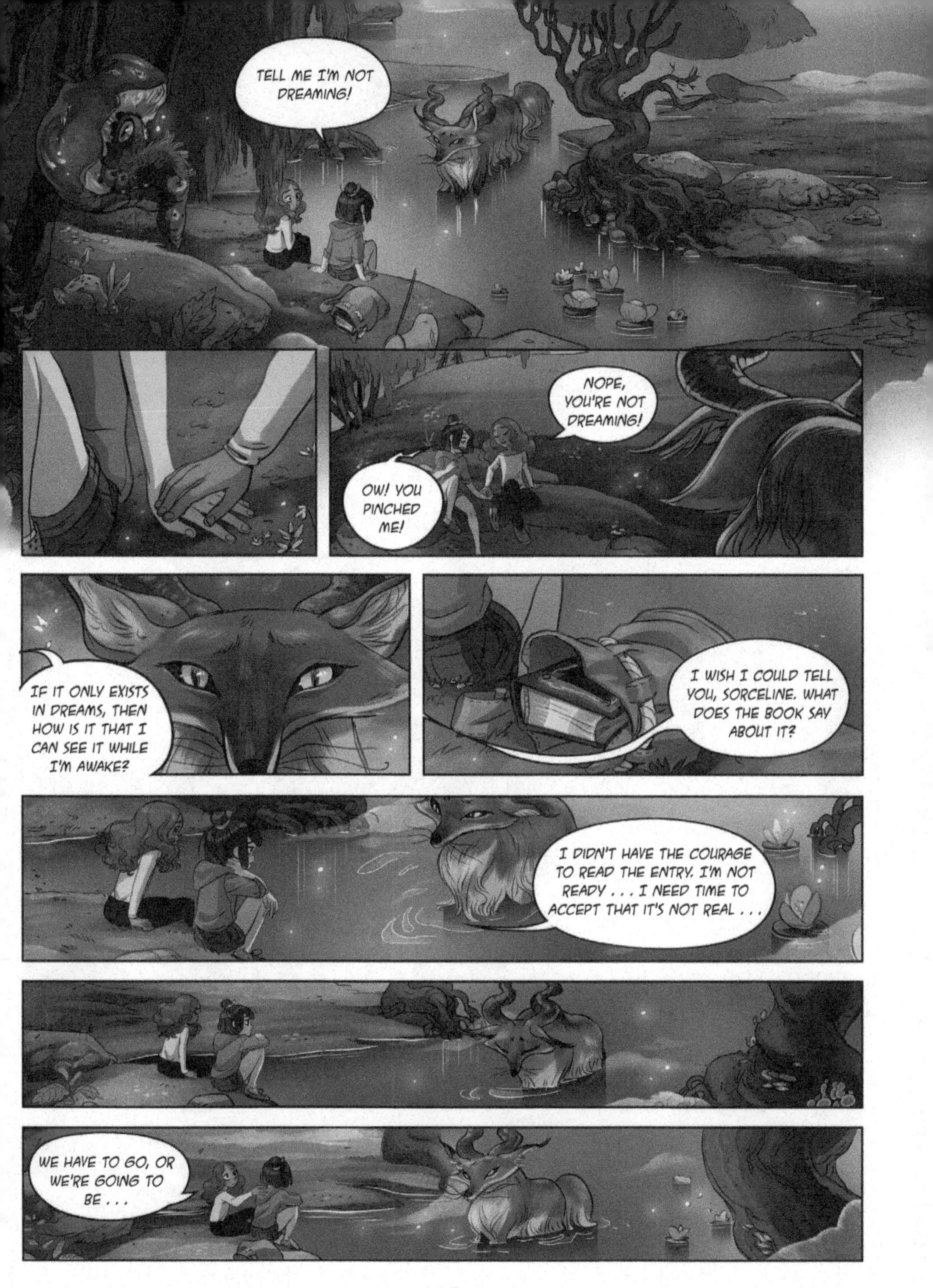
TELL ME I'M NOT DREAMING!
NOPE, YOU'RE NOT DREAMING!
OW! YOU PINCHED ME!
IF IT ONLY EXISTS IN DREAMS, THEN HOW IS IT THAT I CAN SEE IT WHILE I'M AWAKE?
I WISH I COULD TELL YOU, SORCELINE. WHAT DOES THE BOOK SAY ABOUT IT?
I DIDN'T HAVE THE COURAGE TO READ THE ENTRY. I'M NOT READY . . . I NEED TIME TO ACCEPT THAT IT'S NOT REAL . . .
WE HAVE TO GO, OR WE'RE GOING TO BE . . .

LATE! IT'S GETTING TO BE A HABIT!

PROFESSOR BALZAR ISN'T EVEN HERE YET!

NO NEED! I'M TEACHING THE CLASS TODAY!

THANKS TO SORCELINE, YOU ALL KNOW THAT I'M A CRYPTID. THAT'S WHY I'LL BE TEACHING YOU MAGIC.

WHAT'S THAT BOOK?

IT'S CALLED "NONE OF YOUR BUSINESS."

OBVIOUSLY, YOU DON'T HAVE MAGICAL POWERS. YOU ARE NOT SORCERERS . . .

BUT IF YOU WANT TO BECOME CRYPTOZOOLOGISTS, WHETHER YOU SPECIALIZE IN UNICORNS, DRAGONOLOGY, OR FAIRIES . . . YOU WILL NEED TO KNOW HOW TO USE MAGICAL OBJECTS.

EVERYTHING YOU SEE HERE IS MAGIC!

THESE OBJECTS WERE CREATED BY CREATURES WITH SPECIAL POWERS.

AS YOU CAN SEE THERE ARE MANY VARIETIES OF THEM: BRACELETS, CAPES, STONES, GEMS, RINGS . . .

IN ORDER TO USE THEM, YOU NEED TO ACTIVATE THEM.

TO DO THAT, YOU MUST FORM THE APPROPRIATE MAGIC SYMBOLS IN THE AIR, OR IMAGINE THEM . . .

117

HA! HA! HA! HA! HA! HA!

THE SPELLS CAN LAST FROM SEVERAL WEEKS . . .

. . . TO A FEW SECONDS!

OH, OF COURSE!

WHAT?

I JUST UNDERSTOOD SOMETHING!

OOF!

WHY WOULD WE NEED TO USE THAT SPELL?

YOU COULD USE IT TO CAMOUFLAGE YOURSELF WHILE YOU STUDY GNOMO SAPIENS, FOR EXAMPLE.

THEY'RE DISTRUSTFUL CREATURES; HARD TO OBSERVE. THIS DISGUISE COULD ALLOW YOU TO GET CLOSE TO THEM, TO STUDY THEIR CUSTOMS AND BEHAVIOR . . .

I UNDERSTOOD THE SYMBOL TO MEAN "TRANSMUTATION HORRIBUCIO."

YES, THAT'S SORCERIAN, THE LANGUAGE OF SORCERERS.

YOU'RE ABLE TO UNDERSTAND SORCERIAN WITHOUT EVER HAVING STUDIED IT. IT'S A GIFT BESTOWED ON EVERY VISITOR TO THE ISLE OF VORN.

DON'T ASK ME WHY THAT IS . . .

AS LONG AS YOU STAY HERE, YOU WON'T BE ABLE TO REMEMBER!

TARA!

WHAT ARE YOU DOING HERE? WHERE ARE THE OTHERS?

UH . . . I . . . UH . . . IT'S UM . . .

I DON'T HAVE TIME TO DECIPHER YOUR STUTTERING! TELL EVERYONE TO MEET IN THE INFIRMARY. IT'S URGENT!

119

IT'S THE GORGON...

SHE'S DISAPPEARED!

OH, NO!

BUT HOW'S THAT POSSIBLE?

THERE'S ONLY ONE EXPLANATION...

IT'S GOOD AND BAD NEWS!

According to the professor, for some unknown reason, the gorgon got better and left.

While we were happy that the gorgon was healthy, her escape meant an ecological disaster!

SHE COULD TURN EVERY CREATURE SHE ENCOUNTERS INTO STONE!

... she should have been reintroduced into an environment where all the living beings were blind.

120

I HEAR SOMETHING OVER THERE!

WELL, PROFESSOR?

NOTHING HERE!

NOTHING HERE EITHER!

HOW ARE WE GOING TO FIND HER?

I THINK I HAVE AN IDEA!

DO YOU REMEMBER THE FIRST TIME YOU SPOKE TO MERODE IN THE LOCKER ROOM?

YES.

WHAT DID YOU WANT TO TELL HIM ABOUT THE GORGON'S HAIR?

YOU KNOW, I HAVE A WAY OF DEALING WITH HER HAIR. I CAN TELL YOU IF YOU WANT!

OH, YEAH, THAT'S EASY . . .

I just wanted to tell Merode that the way to detangle a gorgon's hair is to play an enchanting melody . . .

. . . on a magic flute.

It will charm the snakes . . .

. . . on the gorgon's head.

Calmed by the music, the snakes unwind . . .

. . . without anyone having to touch them!

IT'S ALSO A GOOD WAY TO ATTRACT A GORGON . . .

Arlene worked hard to learn magic.

NOW WE'RE GOING TO ESTABLISH WHETHER TWO CREATURES ARE PARENT AND CHILD.

JUST WITH THAT MAGIC VIAL?

While we waited for Willa to return, all of us got busy with our various projects.

Tara tried to communicate with her skeleton patient.

"IT'S IDEAL?" OF COURSE IT'S IDEAL FOR ME TO BE HEALING YOU! EVERYONE KNOWS THAT!

And I kept looking for a way to join Willa—even though Professor Balzar had expressly forbidden it.

SORCELINE! I SAID NO ONE WAS TO LEAVE THE MANOR!

BUT PROFESSOR ... THE PIXIE IS SLEEP WALKING AGAIN!

I THINK I SHOULD FOLLOW HER TO SEE WHERE HER DREAMS TAKE HER ...

HMM?

SHE'S MY PATIENT! I NEED TO LOOK AFTER HER, RIGHT?

PLEEAASE.

I HAVE A FEELING I'VE JUST BEEN CONNED . . .

ALL YOU HAVE TO DO IS MIX THE BLOOD OF TWO DISTINCT BEINGS IN THE VIAL . . .

. . . AND THEN ACTIVATE THE MAGIC WITH THE CORRECT SYMBOL.

IF THE LIGHT FROM THE VIAL IS RED, THEY ARE NOT RELATED.

THE LIGHT IS BLUE! THAT MEANS THEY'RE PARENT AND CHILD.

THAT'S AMAZING! I CAN DO MAGIC ON MY OWN!

YOU'RE VERY GIFTED, ARLENE! INCREDIBLY GIFTED!

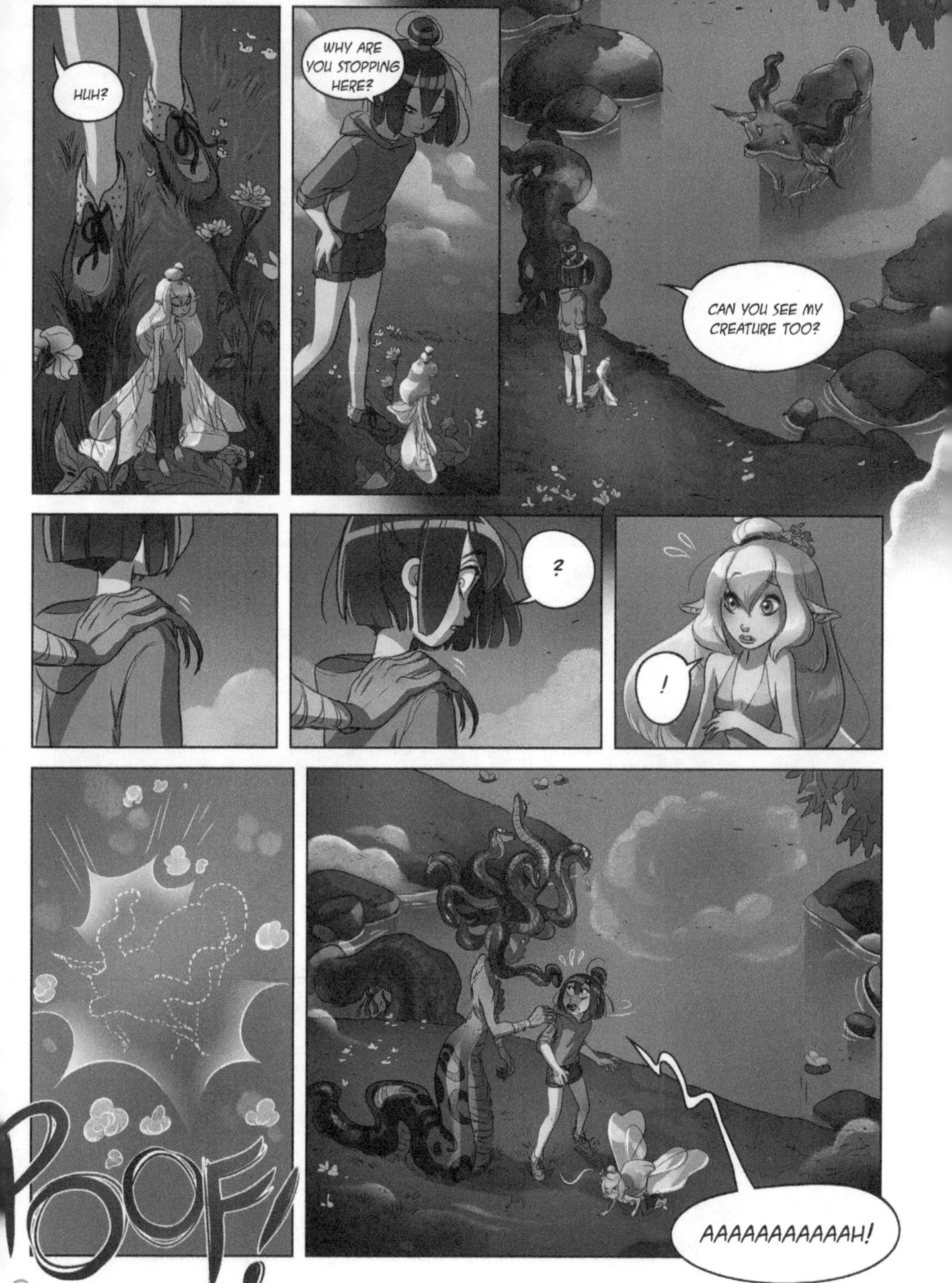
HUH?
WHY ARE YOU STOPPING HERE?
CAN YOU SEE MY CREATURE TOO?
?
!
POOF!
AAAAAAAAAAAH!

SORCELINE!

SORCELINE! YOU OK?

OOF! THANK GOODNESS!

OH NO! THE GORGON!

I . . . THE CREATURE . . . IT VANISHED AND . . .

YOU FAINTED WHEN YOU SAW THE GORGON.

DON'T WORRY! SHE'S HARMLESS! SHE'S BLIND.

BUT LOOK . . .

?

THE PIXIE WAS SCARED STIFF BUT DIDN'T TURN TO STONE WHEN SHE SAW THE GORGON.

INCREDIBLE! SHE'S HAVING THE SAME REACTION TARA DID THIS MORNING!

WHICH MEANS THAT SOME VERSION OF THE GORGON'S POWER HAS BEEN CAUSING THIS!

YES! THE GORGON MUST HAVE BEEN HIDING IN A BUSH OR SOMETHING THIS MORNING AND TARA SAW HER, SO SHE TEMPORARILY FROZE.

SO, MY ORIGINAL HYPOTHESIS WAS CORRECT!

THE PERSON DOING THIS HAS DRAINED A PART OF THE GORGON'S POWER TO PETRIFY THEIR VICTIMS.

BUT REMEMBER, TARA THOUGHT SHE SAW MERODE THIS MORNING! DOES THAT MEAN SHE MISTOOK THE GORGON FOR MERODE? HOW IS THAT POSSIBLE?

AND WHAT IF ALCIDE ISN'T THE GUILTY ONE?

?

IT WAS WHEN I SAW TARA LOOK IN THE MIRROR THAT I UNDERSTOOD!

MERODE WASN'T HOLDING A KNIFE TO DEFEND HIMSELF . . .

HE WAS . . .

HE WAS LOOKING AT HIS REFLECTION IN THE BLADE . . . TO TRANSFORM HIMSELF INTO A STATUE!

THAT'S WHY ALL THE VICTIMS WERE FREED FROM THEIR GLASS PRISONS EXCEPT MERODE! PROFESSOR BALZAR EXPLAINED IT TO US . . .

YOU DO KNOW HOW TO TURN EVERYONE BACK, DON'T YOU?

WELL, YES. WHOEVER IS RESPONSIBLE WILL HAVE TO TURN THEMSELVES INTO A STATUE.

BUT WHY DID HE PETRIFY HIMSELF?

BECAUSE HE'D BEEN PETRIFYING EVERYONE YOU CURSED! YOU CURSED HIM, SO HE HAD TO DO IT TO HIMSELF, TO KEEP YOU THINKING THAT YOU WERE RESPONSIBLE . . .

ARRRRGH!

GRRR, I'M GOING TO SMASH HIM!

YOU CAN'T SMASH HIM! HE'S THE ROOT OF THE WHOLE PROBLEM. IF YOU DO THAT, WE MAY NEVER BE ABLE TO TRANSFORM HIM BACK!

STOP! CALM DOWN!

I DON'T CARE! I WANT HIM TO DISAPPEAR! LET ME GO!

AND MAYBE I'M WRONG AGAIN! WE DON'T KNOW. HE NEEDS A CHANCE TO EXPLAIN HIMSELF . . .

BECAUSE WHAT? YOU THINK HE'LL TELL US THE TRUTH? DREAM ON!

NEVER TRUST ANYONE WHO HIDES ONE OF HIS EYES!

HUH? WHAT DID YOU JUST SAY?

EYES ARE WINDOWS TO THE SOUL! IF ONE EYE IS HIDDEN . . .

OH! THAT'S THE PROOF! THERE'S NO DOUBT ABOUT IT!

OW!

HIS EYE . . .

PROFESSOR, YOU MUST HAVE NOTICED THAT ONE OF MERODE'S EYES WAS ALWAYS COVERED BY HIS BANGS.

We only . . .

. . . ever saw . . .

. . . his left eye.

WELL, LOOK AT MERODE'S STATUE!

THE EVIDENCE WAS RIGHT THERE IN FRONT OF US THE WHOLE TIME!

NOW WE CAN ONLY SEE HIS RIGHT EYE. THE ONE THAT WAS ALWAYS HIDDEN!

EXACTLY! I KNEW THERE WAS SOMETHING DIFFERENT ABOUT HIM.

TO PETRIFY PEOPLE, MERODE SHOWED THEM HIS RIGHT EYE! WE'VE GOT THE PROOF PROFESSOR. HIS RIGHT EYE IS THE WEAPON!

AND THE GORGON WAS CURED BECAUSE ONCE MERODE WAS PETRIFIED, HE NO LONGER HAD CONTROL OVER HER . . .

SHE'LL GET HER SIGHT BACK WHEN MERODE IS NO LONGER A STATUE!

HE MUST HAVE THREATENED HER!

WAIT, PROFESSOR! THERE ARE STILL SOME UNANSWERED QUESTIONS. WHY DIDN'T ALCIDE SAY SOMETHING?

. . . ALCIDE IS NOT A SYLPH, BUT A HUMAN. THAT'S WHY SORCELINE DIDN'T SENSE ANYTHING!

MERODE CLEARLY HAS SOME SUPERNATURAL POWERS SINCE HE WAS ABLE TO STEAL THE GORGON'S MAGIC.

Sorceline sensed Merode's magic when she met him the first time. I'm sure of it now!

OF COURSE! WHY DIDN'T I THINK OF IT SOONER?

?

131

THINK OF WHAT, PROFESSOR?

HMM . . . UH . . . HEE HEE!

I MUST SAY I'M PROUD OF ALL OF YOU! BETWEEN YOU AND THE VERY AMBITIOUS TARA!

THE GORGON IS MY PATIENT NOW. NO ONE TOUCHES HER, OR . . . .

MOM, YOU STILL HAVEN'T ANSWERED MY QUESTION. WAS I ADOPTED?

WHAT DO YOU KNOW ABOUT MERODE AND SORCELINE?

AND ARLENE, WHO, ACCORDING TO MADAME S., IS VERY GIFTED WITH MAGIC . . .

DID YOU KNOW THAT WHEN YOU MIX THE DRAGON'S BLOOD WITH THAT OF A LULLABIS THE RESULT IS PURPLE?

PFFFT! YOU DON'T NEED TO HAVE MAGIC POWERS TO WORK THAT OUT. BLUE + RED = PURPLE!

WHY WON'T YOU ANSWER ME?

ANSWER ME, PROFESSOR!

NOT TO MENTION SORCELINE, WHO HAS HER OWN SPECIAL MAGIC.

DID YOUR FATHER CONTACT YOU?

STOP IT, SORCELINE! STOP PRETENDING THAT YOU HAVE A SIGNAL WHEN YOU KNOW PERFECTLY WELL THAT THERE ISN'T ONE HERE!

EXCUSE ME! I'M TALKING TO MY MOTHER!

BUT LOOK! YOUR PHONE ISN'T EVEN ON, SEE?

HUH? BUT . . . THAT'S REALLY WEIRD . . .

THERE'S NOTHING WEIRD ABOUT IT. YOU'RE JUST LOSING IT!

She may be right. I've lost my mind. That's why I see a creature no one else sees . . .

HEY . . .

THAT'S THE PAGE ABOUT THE CREATURE I SEE . . .

WHY DO YOU HAVE IT?

WHAT? YOU SEE THIS CREATURE IN YOUR DREAMS?

PROFESSOR! SORCELINE IS IN DANGER!

HURRY! WHERE IS SHE?

PROFESSOR! PROFESSOR! WAIT!

SHE'S NOT IN IMMEDIATE DANGER! READ THIS! IT'S ABOUT THE CREATURE SHE SEES!

IS IT TRUE WHAT THEY SAY ABOUT YOU IN THE BOOK?

THAT YOU'RE A BAD OMEN?

NO! IT CAN'T BE!

I'M AFRAID THAT IT'S ALL TRUE . . .

. . . SO, PLEASE! GO! DISAPPEAR! GO!

THIS IS AWFUL!

I TORE OUT THE PAGE SO THAT SORCELINE COULDN'T USE IT. I THOUGHT IT WAS FOR AN ASSIGNMENT . . .

IT DOESN'T MATTER WHAT TARA DID!

NO WAY! YOU WANTED TO SABOTAGE HER WORK AGAIN?!

NOTHING MATTERS ANYMORE.

SORCELINE IS . . . SHE'S GONNA . . .

DIE!

I'M GOING TO DIE IF YOU DON'T GET OUT OF MY SIGHT!

The Omen

Free it or die! If you see him in your dreams, death awaits you! To avoid your fate, you must banish this creature.

YOU'RE GOING TO SAVE SORCELINE, RIGHT, PROFESSOR?

I'M NOT SURE ANY OF US CAN...

WHEN YOU SEE THE OMEN, YOU'RE IN SERIOUS TROUBLE...

SORCELINE SAID THAT THE ONE SHE SEES IS STUCK IN THE WATER.

SHE NEEDS TO FIND A WAY TO GET IT OUT OF THE WATER...

I CAN'T DO IT!

SO, I'M DOOMED?

THERE'S ONLY ONE THING LEFT TO DO...

RUN FROM MY FATE!

I NEED TO GET OFF THIS ISLAND!

IT MUST ALSO HAVE TO DO WITH HOW WE LEAVE . . .

ACCORDING TO MADAME S., SORCERIAN—THE LANGUAGE OF SORCERERS—HAS SOMETHING TO DO WITH HOW WE ALL ARRIVED ON THE ISLE OF VORN . . .

?

THIS BOOK IS WRITTEN IN SORCERIAN . . .

YES, NOW I REMEMBER . . .

LIBRARY

This book is the portal! I found it in the town library . . .

I was immediately drawn to it.

It explained how to get to an island full of fantastical creatures...

But I didn't realize that I was the only one who could read it. I didn't even realize it was written in Sorcerian...

OH? THIS BOOK ISN'T TAKEN OUT MUCH! I DON'T UNDERSTAND A WORD OF IT! WHAT LANGUAGE IS IT IN?

In order to get to the Isle of Vorn, you must read this book until you come to the words that put you to sleep...

READ THOSE WORDS, AND YOU WILL FIND YOUR WAY TO THE ISLAND.

As soon as you read them, you will doze off, and your sleep will guide you on your journey...

You will wake up on the island without knowing how you arrived!

But it's not a dream! When you are on the island, you are not asleep in your bed.

It's just that you will not remember the journey because you don't remember the moment when you fell asleep. Only when you wake will you realize that you dozed off.

You must have to read the book backwards to go back...

SORCELINE? I JUST HEARD THE TERRIBLE NEWS!

I'M HERE FOR YOU. YOU KNOW THAT, RIGHT?

?

THIS IS WHAT THE OMEN PREDICTED...

GRAVE DANGER...

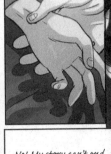

No! My story can't end like this! I came here to become a healer... not a patient!

PROBABLY A SERIOUS ILLNESS... DEADLY EVEN!

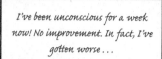

I've been unconscious for a week now! No improvement. In fact, I've gotten worse...

THE PROFESSOR SAID WE NEED TO CHECK EVERYONE'S BLOOD TO COMPARE BLOOD TYPES WITH SORCELINE!

OH, QUIT WHINING!

OW.

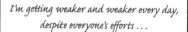

I'm getting weaker and weaker every day, despite everyone's efforts...

IF SHE NEEDS BLOOD, IT'LL BE MINE THAT'LL SAVE HER!

PFF, I DON'T THINK YOUR SNAKE'S BLOOD IS GOING TO HELP!

I'M AFRAID THAT YOU NEED TO PREPARE YOURSELVES TO SAY GOODBYE TO SORCELINE...

THERE'S NOTHING MORE WE CAN DO...

BUT WAIT! ONE OF US CAN STILL GIVE HER BLOOD LIKE YOU SUGGESTED...

WE NEED TO LET HER GO, WILLA...

I'M GOING TO HER ROOM TO GATHER HER THINGS.

HEY, TARA, THAT'S FOR ME TO DO!

GIVE ME THAT VIAL!

YOU SEE, YOU DON'T HAVE A GIFT FOR MAGIC!

BUT YOU MIXED UP THE VIALS! YOU USED THE ONE FOR FAMILY RELATIONSHIPS, NOT THE ONE FOR BLOOD TYPES.

I'LL SHOW YOU MY GIFT! WHEN I FORM THIS SYMBOL, THE RED LIGHT WILL APPEAR . . .

. . . SINCE NONE OF US ARE PARENT AND CHILD!

BUT . . . HEY! IT'S BLUE! WHOSE BLOOD DID YOU MIX?!

141

The real tragedy is that I'm about to die far from home, without the company of my family. It's a pity I don't realize that, right by my side is . . .

. . . my real mother!

TO BE CONTINUED IN THE NEXT INSTALLMENT OF

Sorceline

Andrews McMeel Publishing
a division of Andrews McMeel Universal
1130 Walnut Street, Kansas City, Missouri 64106

www.andrewsmcmeel.com

Published in French by Editions Glénat as three volumes:

Original Title: *Sorceline – tome 01 : Un jour je serai fantasticologue!*
Authors: Sylvia Douyé (Text) & Paola Antista (Artwork)
© Editions Glénat 2018 – ALL RIGHTS RESERVED

Original Title: *Sorceline – tome 02 : La fille qui aimait les animonstres*
Authors: Sylvia Douyé (Text) & Paola Antista (Artwork)
© Editions Glénat 2019 – ALL RIGHTS RESERVED

Original Title: *Sorceline – tome 03 : Au cœur de mes zoorigines*
Authors: Sylvia Douyé (Text) & Paola Antista (Artwork)
© Editions Glénat 2020 – ALL RIGHTS RESERVED

22 23 24 25 26 SDB 10 9 8 7 6 5 4 3 2 1

ISBN: 978-1-5248-7131-4

Library of Congress Control Number: 2021948437

ATTENTION: SCHOOLS AND BUSINESSES
Andrews McMeel books are available at quantity discounts with bulk purchase for educational, business, or sales promotional use. For information, please e-mail the Andrews McMeel Publishing Special Sales Department: specialsales@amuniversal.com.